Diving Adventure

DIVING

Willard Price

ADVENTURE

The John Day Company · New York

The John Day Company, 257 Park Avenue South, New York, N.Y. 10010
an Intext *publisher*

Published on the same day in Canada by Longmans Canada Limited.

Library of Congress Catalogue Card Number:70-117170
Printed in the United States of America
Design by The Etheredges

Contents

About This Book

This story is fiction, and Undersea City belongs to the future, not the present. But many incidents in the story are based upon actual adventures in Jacques Cousteau's village on the floor of the Red Sea, the U.S. Navy's Sealabs off California, Japan's seaweed and pearl farms, oil wells in the Gulf of Mexico, sunken cities of Greece and Jamaica, underwater parks of Florida and the West Indies, the submarine town at Monaco, and the author's underwater experiences in the Bahamas and South Pacific. Well over a thousand scientific and industrial enterprises are already under way on the sea floor.

Man has proved that he can make himself at home beneath the sea and harvest its untold riches.

Undersea City

About to descend to the sea bottom, they strapped on their face masks, scuba tanks, weighted belts, and fins.

"Ready?" asked Dr. Dick.

"Ready," Hal said.

Ready for the great adventure.

Hal Hunt and his younger brother, Roger, had made many dives in the past, but never to an underwater city. They looked over the rail of the research ship, *Discovery*, but could not see to the bottom. The idea that there were streets, houses, parks, factories down below seemed fantastic.

"Over we go," said Dr. Dick, and they dropped from the deck into the tropical waters of the Great Barrier Reef.

They sank rapidly through shoals of brightly colored angelfish. Deeper, the many colors merged into a rich blue. They began to see the roofs of Undersea City. They felt like aviators winging down from the sky to a busy town.

Dr. Dick began to swim and signed to them to follow. He led them to a broad avenue and they slowly dropped into it, until their feet touched the ground two hundred feet below the surface of the Pacific. A sign told them that this was Main Street. They half walked, half swam, among other men who were doing the same.

All were light on their feet. In fact, it was a little difficult to stay on the sea floor. They floated rather than walked.

The weight of the lead in their belts held them down, but was nearly offset by the density of the water. The result was that the least extra pressure of a foot against the earth sent them soaring like birds.

Mischief-loving Roger could not refrain from trying out his powers of flight. With a sudden push of his foot he bounced himself upward a dozen feet and came down like an acrobat to stand on Hal's shoulders.

Hal, surprised, unable to see straight above him because of the mask, didn't know what had struck him. It might be a dangerous fish. He reached up to push it away. His hand encountered Roger's ankle.

He closed his hand on the ankle, brought the rascal down, turned him over, and stood him on his head. Dr. Dick looked on with tolerant amusement as the boy got back on his feet.

At the corner of Main and Research Streets Dr. Dick stopped at a house somewhat larger than the others. Like all the rest, it stood on stilts about seven feet high. There were no steps up to the front door—in fact, there was no front door. Dr. Dick went beneath the building. Then with a thrust of his fins, he sent himself up until his head went through a hole in the floor. He clambered up into the house. The boys followed.

There was no water in the house. The boys and their leader removed their masks and tanks.

Roger's eyes were wide open in disbelief. He stared at the hole in the floor.

"Why doesn't the water come up into the house?" he squeaked.

Hal laughed. "You sound like Donald Duck," he said. But so did he.

Dr. Dick smiled. "You'll have to learn to keep your voices low. The reason they are so high is that the air supplied to the houses down here is not like the air you breathe up above. There, it has a lot of oxygen and nitrogen in it. At this depth so much of those gases would be poisonous. Here you are breathing mostly helium and it's the 'squeak gas'—but you'll soon learn to talk low.

"Now, you asked why doesn't the water come up into the house. It's because we keep the air pressure in the house exactly the same as the water pressure outside."

Roger looked blank.

On a side table was a pitcher of drinking water. Dr. Dick took a glass, turned it over, pressed the open end down into the water.

"You see what happens," he said. "No water goes up into the glass. The air in the glass keeps out the water. Every house, office, and shop in town is kept dry in the same way. So long as the air is as strong as the water, the water is kept out. There's a dressing room yonder. You'll find towels and some dry clothes."

The boys stripped off their gear and bathing suits, toweled themselves dry, and dressed. They came out to find the living room empty. Dr. Dick called to them from another room. They went into what appeared to be an office. Dr. Dick sat behind a large desk.

Alan Dick was a kindly man, with a twinkle in his eye, but looked just what he was—a distinguished doctor of science, Director of the Undersea Science Foundation which had built Undersea City and was in charge of its many experiments.

"Well," he said, "how do you like it in our new world?"

"It's amazing," Hal said. "A very strange world to us. Perhaps you'd better start by briefing us on what we are supposed to do."

Treasures of the Sea Bottom

"Let me tell you first," said Dr. Dick, "what we are trying to accomplish here. Then I'll tell you how you fit in. We're here to study the best ways to use the fabulous riches of the sea.

"The world needs these riches. The land is not producing enough. After all, only one quarter of the world is land. All the rest is sea. We have dug out of the land a large part of the valuable metals. You don't hear any more about a Gold Rush in California or Australia—the gold is gone.

"The silver mines are being exhausted. Copper mines are dying out. There is a severe shortage of magnesium. A single big airplane needs a ton of it. There are five million tons of magnesium in every cubic mile of seawater.

"Manganese is necessary to make steel. Much of the sea floor is covered with potato-shaped lumps of manganese.

"There's plenty of nickel and cobalt in the sea. There are great reservoirs of oil beneath the sea floor. There are vast stores of potash, platinum, titanium, sulfur, zinc, uranium, bromine, tin, and diamonds."

"Why isn't something being done about it?" Hal asked.

"Why aren't the mining companies interested?"

"They are," said Dr. Dick. "Deeply interested. Many British and Russian firms and more than a thousand American companies are digging the sea bottom. They want to know how to do it better. Some of the big ones are paying us to find out. That's the reason our Undersea Science Foundation was formed."

"And now tell us what we can do to help," Hal said.

"In a way," said Dr. Dick, "your job is the most important of all. There's just one thing that the world needs more than metals."

"And what is that?"

"Food. Eighty percent of all animal life is in the sea. And ninety percent of the vegetation. And yet only one percent of human food comes from the sea. That's a problem for naturalists like you. How can we get more out of the sea? How can we make the sea produce the kinds of food that people like? We have something to learn from the Orientals. The Chinese have been running fish farms for centuries. The Japanese make seaweed farms—seaweed is a good food. They grow millions of oysters in their oyster beds. And the oysters produce millions of cultured pearls that bring a good price all over the world.

"Whales should be protected so they can breed freely. The meat and oil of one whale is worth thirty thousand dollars. The Lapps don't go out in the wilds when they want a reindeer. They raise their own. We don't depend upon finding a wild sheep when we want some mutton. We have our flocks. We cultivate the earth. Why not cultivate the sea?"

Hal's eyes were shining. "Now I begin to see what you want of us."

"Of course you do," Dr. Dick smiled. "We've followed your career with interest. Your father is a famous collector of animals and has sent you to many parts of the world to take land animals and creatures of the sea alive for zoos and aquariums, so you have had a lot of experience as a naturalist. And we need a naturalist to head up these studies."

"But why me?" Hal asked. "There are many naturalists much older and more experienced." Hal wished at that moment that he was a lot more than nineteen years of age.

"You have more experience," Dr. Dick said, "out in the wilds than a naturalist twice your age gets in the laboratory with his eye glued to a microscope. Don't be ashamed of your youth. It's just what we need—work undersea is much tougher than up yonder and takes plenty of physical strength and endurance." He looked Hal over. "You look as if you could stand the gaff. And your brother, too. How old are you, Roger?"

"Fourteen."

"Big for your age. You look as if you could take on a gorilla single-handed. You both understand the arrangement I made with your father. Besides helping us, you will be allowed to collect rare fish for his aquariums. So your career as take-'em-alive men will not be interrupted. Of course we will provide you with food and lodging. Perhaps you would like to see now where you will live. Your cottage is just around the corner on Barracuda Street. Let's go."

Changing back into their diving gear, they dropped through the "front door" and swam around to Barracuda Street.

Home Beneath the Sea

Entering their cottage through the hole in the floor, the boys found themselves in a comfortable living room that opened into a kitchen, bath, and two bedrooms.

"How do you like it?" Dr. Dick asked.

"It's groovy," Roger exclaimed.

"Wonderful," said Hal. "Who would ever imagine a place like this at the bottom of the sea! But we don't need so much space. Two bedrooms—one would be enough."

"And one will be all you will have," Dr. Dick said. "You see, there isn't enough housing to go around, so it's necessary for us to double up a bit. I hope you don't object to sharing your cottage."

"Not at all," Hal said. "In fact, we'll enjoy having company."

"I think you'll find Mr. Kaggs good company," said the director. "He's a well-educated man of the highest moral principles."

Hal knitted his brows. "What did you say his name was?"

"Kaggs."

Hal was trying to remember. "Is he—a preacher?"

"Why, yes. How did you know? The Reverend Merlin Kaggs. He's the pastor of our church."

"Merlin Kaggs," exclaimed Hal. "Yes, we know him."

"Fine. That makes it all the better. Since you are already friends, you should get along very well together."

Hal thought bitterly, I'd rather share the cottage with a snake. But something kept him from saying it.

Roger was not so discreet. "Isn't that the guy who—"

"Pipe down," said Hal sharply.

He, or Roger, could ruin Kaggs's reputation with ten words. Kaggs was no holy man. He was a criminal with two murders to his credit. He pretended to be a missionary, went about with his hands clasped in prayer, and quoted the Bible while plotting to steal and kill. He had schemed to steal a pearl farm, and because the boys stood in his way he had left them to die on a desert island.* Yes, Hal remembered the "Reverend" Merlin Kaggs only too well.

But perhaps the rascal had reformed. Dr. Dick thought well of him. He was honored in this submarine community. Hal was no tattletale. He believed in giving every man the benefit of the doubt. He must keep quiet—at least until he had had a chance to talk with the fellow and find out whether he was the thief and killer he had always been, or was now a new man.

Thinking these thoughts, he stood by a Plexiglas window looking out into the strangest street he had ever seen—a street swarming with fish.

"What made you choose this spot for your town?" he asked Dr. Dick.

The director came to the window. "There's part of your answer," he said, nodding at the fish. "Sea life is more plenti-

*As told in *South Sea Adventure*.

ful in tropical waters than anywhere else. And coral reefs attract fish. They eat the coral animals and they love to hide in the holes in the reef. The Great Barrier is the largest coral reef in the whole world— 1,250 miles long—and harbors the world's richest sea life. The sea floor is full of minerals. So it's the ideal place for a study of oceanic resources."

Roger was peering out the window. "What's that small building behind the cottage?"

"That, my boy, should be of special interest to you. That's your garage. Your car has already been parked in it."

"My car?"

"Well, not exactly. Underwater, it's better than a car. Really, a diving boat. You're our official errand boy, you know. You will carry messages, tools, and supplies from one part of the town to another. You know how to drive a car?"

"Of course."

"Then you'll have no trouble with the glass jeep."

"Glass? How could it be glass?"

"Something new," said Dr. Dick. "Other diving boats are made of steel—the Diving Saucer, Deep Star, Deep Diver, Midget Sub, Cachalot, Sunfish, and the rest. This is the first to be made of glass."

"Why glass? I should think glass would break."

"On the contrary, glass will resist sea pressure better than steel. The more you compress it, the stronger it becomes. Also, it has some fiberglass and plastic in it. Naturally, it's much lighter than steel. And salt water doesn't corrode it, so it can stay underwater for weeks or years without damage. And the most wonderful thing about it is that you can see through it—ahead, behind, up, down, everywhere."

"Great," Hal said. "Who was smart enough to invent that?"

"The first was built by a physicist named McLean—the same man who invented the air-to-air missile. Director of the

Naval Ordnance Test Station. He was awarded the Rockefeller Public Service Award of ten thousand dollars for his invention. Ours is not like the original. We have improved it a lot for our own use. But it's still glass."

"Will it actually go deep without breaking?" Hal wanted to know.

"We think it can go to the deepest trenches of the ocean, 36,000 feet down—nearly seven miles. That seems hard to believe, doesn't it? It hasn't been tested yet at such depths. Anybody who wants to take his life in his hands can go down with it that deep and see what happens. I wouldn't care to be the one. Here's a manual that tells you how to operate it." He handed Roger a small booklet. "And now if you will excuse me I must get back to the office."

Roger studied the manual, then popped out to the garage to examine the glass jeep.

Hal, left alone, thought sourly about Kaggs, thought happily about the work that lay ahead of him.

Roger came back full of enthusiasm. "Greatest thing you ever saw. Want to take a spin?"

Hal was a little apprehensive. "Sure you can manage it?"

"It doesn't look too difficult. Let's try it out."

The Glass Jeep

It was the strangest garage they had ever seen. It was open to the sea and full of water. A large window in the roof let in light.

At first Hal could see no glass boat. Then he realized that he was looking straight through it. It had just enough positive buoyancy to hold it against the roof of the garage.

It was like the house: the "front door" was a hole in the bottom.

The glass diving boat resembled a large egg, about six feet long. The small end was the bow. There was a low seat in the rear for the two occupants. The boat looked rather like a large shiny bug because the four short jet pipes projecting from it were like legs, and a jointed arm stretched out ahead with jaws at the end ready to bite. This was the "grab" that could be used to seize objects, animals or fish.

They swam up and crawled in through the hole. The inside was dry and full of air. Roger closed the hatch.

"How do you get it out of the garage?" Hal asked. "I don't see any propeller."

"It works by jets—something like a jet plane." Roger was in his element. He enjoyed teaching his elder brother. "Each of those pipes is a jet, but they spout water instead of air. So they're called hydrojets. 'Hydro' means water."

"Yes, I know," said Hal impatiently. "Get on with it."

"The rear jets push the thing forward. The left forward jet turns the bow to the right. The right jet turns the bow to the left. You can go up by pointing both forward jets down. You go down by pointing them up. You can even back up—by turning the back jets off and pointing the front jets straight forward."

"Yes, but how do you operate these jets?"

"Simple. See this lever? Push it up and you go up. Down, and you go down. Left, you go left, and right, you go right. Over here into reverse, and you go back."

"And that button?"

"That works the grab. Pull it out and the jaws open. Push in and the jaws close."

"Sounds pretty simple," admitted Hal. "I wonder if it's as simple as you think. Let's go."

Roger started the motor. The glass jeep slid out of the garage and headed straight for the next house.

"Look out, we're going to crash."

Roger seized the steering lever. In his excitement, he pushed it the wrong way. The boat plunged toward the downstairs window.

In a panic, he jammed the lever to the right. The jeep turned smartly right, and threatened to take off the heads of some of the men passing along the street. Roger pushed the lever up and the jeep climbed like a scared cat.

It taught Roger two things. One, be sure you know what you're doing. Two, this jeep was like something alive. It could turn on a dime, shoot up like a meteor, drop like a falling star.

"It beats a car forty ways," he said.

Now they were passing over the roofs of Undersea City. All the roofs were flat; they did not need to be gabled, since they never had to shed rain or snow. Both the roofs and the walls were covered by seaweed and mollusks, food for the thousands of fish. Clouds of fish parted before the bow of the glass jeep.

Columns of bubbles rose from the buildings and from the aqualungs of swimmers and pedestrians. A building marked AIR was evidently the point from which pressurized helium breathing gas was distributed by underground conduits.

There, with a small spire, was the church of which the rascally Reverend Merlin Kaggs was pastor. Roger could hardly resist the temptation to nip off the spire. He high-jumped over it.

The jeep skimmed over what appeared to be a power plant turning out electricity to supply the town with light and heat.

There was a building that Hal guessed might be a desalting plant to turn salt water into fresh and distribute it around town.

There were streets of residences, green with tropical growth. The houses were set in pleasant gardens with the most fantastic and beautiful plants—and animals that looked like plants—sea fans, coral trees, sea anemones, gorgeous gorgonias, waxy little animal flowers like tulips.

The principal shopping street appeared to be Main where shops had windows but no doors. Stilts anchored them to the ground and the entrances were underneath. People floated up into them and came out with plastic bags of groceries and household articles.

There was a dairy that advertised whale's milk, a bookstore announcing "Books on the Underworld," a restaurant, a barber shop, a shop that offered "Deep-down Souvenirs," a hospital, a pharmacy, a bank, and a shop where one could buy "Jewels from the Seabed."

A man came out of a hardware store with a piece of iron machinery as big as himself.

"Golly," exclaimed Roger. "That thing must weigh half a ton."

"Up above, it would," Hal said. "Down here, he can carry it easily because the dense water helps hold it up."

There was even a pet shop—but the pets were not dogs, cats, and canaries. They were dolphins, porpoises, and ornamental fish.

And there were several shops specializing in diving gear, scuba tanks patterned after Cousteau's aqualung, fins, masks, snorkels, and everything else the well-dressed underwater man would wear.

Now the scene changed. Here was a lovely underwater park with paths winding between the "trees," brain coral, corals like minarets, starfish, wonderful shells, giant clams, and other strange and beautiful sights of the seabed.

On the edge of town was the industrial district where experiments in mining were going on. The sea floor was being explored by men with magnetometers that would detect any metals below the surface. Ore containing gold, silver, uranium, magnesium, and other buried treasure was being lifted to the ship above by electromagnets.

Roger throttled down the motor and drifted slowly over a great iron seesaw rocking back and forth like a teeterboard. "What's that?"

"A pump bringing up oil," Hal said. "You've seen them in the Gulf of Mexico."

"But there they were up on platforms over the sea."

"Yes, but that's a very poor way to bring up oil from the sea floor. It's terribly expensive to reach down so far to get at the well. Besides, it's extremely dangerous—the platform may be torn down by a typhoon or rammed by a ship. Great waves may destroy it. It's far better to get right down where the well is and escape all the things that can happen up on the surface. Watch out—there's something dead ahead."

Roger turned the glass jeep just in time to escape crashing into a towering cliff.

"It's the reef," exclaimed Hal. "The Great Barrier Reef itself."

The precipice rose as straight as the wall of a skyscraper. This was the greatest structure ever built by living creatures. It was greater than the pyramids of Egypt, greater than the Aswan Dam, greater than the Great Wall of China. It was 1,250 miles long, stretching from one end to the other of the Coral Sea, walling in the east coast of Australia. And this colossal structure had been built by one of the smallest of builders, the coral animal so small that it was hard to see it without a microscope.

This part of the great Pacific had been quite properly named the Coral Sea because it afforded the finest display of coral to be found in all the world.

The coral cliff was the home of millions of fish. Some with hard-as-rock snouts battered off chunks and ate them. Countless small fish of every color shot into caves and crevices in its surface to escape big fish-eating fish determined to devour them. Sharks were so numerous that the boys were glad to be protected, although they felt terribly exposed with nothing between them and these predators but a plate of glass. Moray eels and octopuses made their homes in holes. A writhing sea snake coiled around one of the jets. Sea anemones, clinging to the wall, stretched out their tentacles to sting any hand that might touch them or paralyze any small fish that might come within reach. Barracuda with open jaws rushed in to get a closer look at the boys and appeared much surprised when they banged into something they could not see.

Altogether, it was a bit terrifying. But suddenly a more friendly creature appeared. It was a dolphin, and the boys knew that the dolphin was the friend and protector of man.

The dolphin had a pointed, bottle-shaped nose. In that way it differed from the porpoise, which had a blunt, rounded nose. Both, like man, must come to the surface to breathe. But unlike man, who cannot hold his breath for more than three minutes, they could stay down some thirty minutes at a time.

They were like man in another way. They were intelligent. Along with their air-breathing cousins such as whales, they were the most intelligent creatures of the sea except man— who also must be reckoned now as a creature of the sea.

The dolphin, peering into the glass jeep, seemed to be smiling. The smile might be just the natural turn-up of the corners of the mouth, but it gave the boys confidence that here was someone who would never do them harm and just might become a good and faithful companion.

If anyone could win him over, Roger could. He had a way with animals. So had Hal. But Hal was so big and powerful that animals were a little afraid of him. They seemed to feel that they had nothing to fear from his young brother.

Roger turned off the motor and drifted. He tapped on the glass.

"Hi there, Mr. Bottle. Come over and say howdy-do. You're the finest gentleman in the sea. Come and get acquainted."

He kept on talking quietly and the dolphin seemed to be listening. "I don't suppose he can really hear me," Roger said.

"He can hear you."

"I don't see any ears."

"He has ears, but they are very small. He does most of his hearing without ears."

"How can you hear without ears?"

"You can't," Hal said. "But the dolphin can. Sound makes vibrations in the air or water. Delicate nerves in the skin of the dolphin feel these vibrations. Different sounds make different kinds of vibrations, and the dolphin can tell one from another. The sound doesn't have to be strong. Scientific tests have shown that even the splash of a falling drop of water causes a dolphin to turn his head in that direction and look. He knows pretty well what is going on around him at all times."

The dolphin was talking back. His speech was a sort of whistle and sounded friendly. It came not from his mouth, but from the blowhole in the top of his head.

"The dolphin has no vocal cords," Hal said. "But he has a big vocabulary just the same. They've made tape recordings of the dolphin's whistles and they find he has thirty-two different kinds of whistle. Each one means something different. Friendliness, fear, anger, weariness, pleasure, distress, a cry for help, and so on."

"Well," Roger said, "that's one way the dolphin is not like us. No human beings talk in whistles."

"That's where you're wrong," his brother said. "The bushmen of Africa talk in whistles. So do certain tribes in the Amazon jungle. Some Mexican Indians use whistle language, but can't express as many different ideas and feelings with it as the dolphin can. In the Pyrenees there is a whistling speech. Canary Island shepherds on mountain peaks three miles apart talk with each other in a whistling language.

"And the dolphin has another language—a language of clicks. It's not every human being that knows two languages. But the dolphin does. Dolphins that have been around human beings develop a third language—an imitation of the speech of the humans. In an oceanarium they get to understand what their trainer tells them to do, and they try to repeat what he says. They don't do too well with it because of the lack of vocal cords. But they understand it well enough to follow instructions. They even learn to answer in a low-enough voice so that they can be heard."

"What do you mean, low-enough voice? Can't you hear a high voice?"

"Not if it's too high for our ears. Sound is measured in kilocycles. A man can't hear any sound above 20 kilocycles. A dog can hear up to 40 kilocycles. A bottlenose dolphin can hear sounds above 120 kilocycles. He can make sounds that high, but it doesn't take him long to notice that his human friend doesn't hear them. Most of his talk to his fellow dolphins is up in that range, but he learns that he must get his voice down if he wants to talk with us. He must think us pretty stupid."

"I wish we had some fish to feed him," Roger said. "Then perhaps he'd stick around."

"That would help," said Hal. "But it isn't really necessary. You have to feed a cat or dog if you want to keep it. But a dolphin may stay with you just because he likes humans. You've seen them gamboling along beside a ship. They're not looking for food, but just want to play and enjoy the admiration of those creatures up on deck that they seem to think are very much like them.

"And so we are. They breathe air, and so do we. They don't wear scales as the fish do, but have skins as smooth as ours. They have very highly developed brains, and we think we have too. We are built more or less alike. We are mammals, and so are they. We lived on land for ages, and so did they. They once walked. They took to the sea again, but if you take a dolphin apart you find that what are now fins were once legs and all the joints are still there, including five complete fingers. We don't know why they decided to go back to the sea, but today man also is going back to the sea—at least you and I are, and thousands or millions will in the future."

"Look—a moray," Roger said, pointing at a greenish-black tail projecting from a hole in the precipice.

The dolphin saw it, too, and at once undertook to capture the vicious moray eel, a choice meal for a dolphin.

Mr. Bottle's jaws closed on the tail, then he paddled strongly backward, trying to dislodge the snakelike creature from its retreat.

Roger thought Mr. Bottle would win easily, for he appeared to weigh about four hundred pounds and the moray would not tip the scales at a hundred.

But the more the dolphin pulled, the tighter the eel wound itself into the rock crevice. Its muscles expanded and gripped the walls of the crack so firmly that it could not be pulled loose.

Mr. Bottle had to give up and go to the surface for a breath of air. Then he came down and lay contemplating the moray, tilting his head to one side as if thinking things over.

A scorpion fish swam lazily out of the next hole. The scorpion fish is one of the most venomous inhabitants of the sea. The dolphin eyed it thoughtfully.

Then he chased it, swept down below it, and came up like a thunderbolt to plunge his hard bottle nose into the fish's belly. One blow was enough to kill the fish.

Then the dolphin seized the scorpion fish by the belly and jammed the poisoned spines into the moray's tail.

The moray relaxed like a punctured balloon and was easily pulled out of its hole. It was six feet long—six feet of good eating.

The performance gave a good idea of the almost manlike brain of the dolphin. He knew the scorpion fish had poisonous spines. He also knew he needed a tool to dislodge the eel. He didn't seize the fish by the back where the spines were but on the underside where there were no spines. He used this deadly tool to kill the moray eel.

"I can't believe my eyes," Roger said.

"You can believe them," said Hal. "Exactly the same thing happened in the fish tank of Marineland of the Pacific near Los Angeles. Spectators looking in through the glass windows on the side of the tank saw the whole act."

The glass jeep now floated lazily, without movement, near the coral cliff. The dolphin returned from his meal to rub his nose against the glass just where Roger's fingers were tapping it.

"It looks as if he'd like to get closer," Roger said. "Would it be all right to open the hatch?"

"Why not? Go ahead."

Roger dropped the hatch. Immediately the dolphin swam beneath, poked his nose up into the jeep, and whistled a friendly greeting. The jaws were open and the teeth looked sharp. Roger, a little timidly, reached down and stroked the creature's neck much as he would have petted the neck of a dog or cat. The dolphin made a series of soft clicks almost like a purr.

Mr. Bottle and the Tiger

This happy scene was interrupted by a savage visitor. A huge tiger shark that had been swimming around idly at some distance, minding his own business, suddenly became interested in that open hatch. He came over at full speed, pushed Mr. Bottle out of the way, and thrust his whole head up into the jeep. His jaws also were open, but how different they were from those of the dolphin. They were armed not with one row but with five rows of deadly teeth, the largest and most terrible being in front, the others getting smaller, the last row far back in the jaw not more than a half inch long and only sharp enough to tear a man to pieces.

The shark is believed to be the only animal with five semicircles of teeth. They all tilt backward so that once they grip their prey it cannot pull loose. The teeth are so keen-edged that they are used by primitive tribes as razors for shaving. They have been known to cut a man in two at a single bite.

The shark is believed to have been the first creature to grow teeth. Later they were adopted by the bony fishes, amphibians, reptiles, mammals, and humans. Even the great tusks of the elephant go back to the shark's invention of teeth.

The shark liked teeth so well that it was not satisfied to have them just in its mouth. It grew them all over its body. The scales of the shark are really teeth. Every scale is pointed and sharp like a tooth, made of the same material, covered by dentin, and has a central pulp canal containing a nerve.

These denticles give the tough hides of most sharks a roughness like that of sandpaper that can scratch or tear a swimmer's flesh. In fact, before sandpaper was invented, shark hide called *shagreen* was used by carpenters to smooth hard wood. The teeth are so large and close to one another that it is difficult to drive a harpoon into the hide. Even bullets bounce off.

But the best, or worst, of the teeth are in the mouth. Why five rows? The shark is a tremendous eater—it may use its teeth a hundred times in a day. As the front teeth wear out, the row just behind moves up to the front and another row begins to form far back in the mouth. The result is that the shark always has good teeth no matter how long it may live.

"I never saw such teeth," Roger said. "The front ones must be four inches long."

"Shark's teeth are the largest in the fish world," said Hal. "After all, they've taken a long time to evolve. Fossil shark teeth are found in rock 130,000,000 years old. And they are very much like those of today. So it must have been many millions of years before that when the earliest sharks began to be equipped with teeth."

"I don't see any molars," Roger said. "All the teeth appear to be cutters."

"You're right," said Hal. "They don't grind. They slice like a knife. The lion has terrible teeth but they can't compare with a shark's. The lion has to chew and worry at a carcass to get a mouthful, but a blue shark or tiger or mako can slide up to a victim in the sea and spoon off ten pounds without slowing down. Its teeth go through hide and flesh and muscle as if they were soft ice cream."

"Shark bite must hurt like the dickens."

"Strangely enough," Hal said, "it may not hurt a bit. It happens so quickly and is so clean that it may not be felt until later. The nerves don't have time to talk back. A Malay pearl diver swam up to his boat and said to his friends, 'I don't know whether a shark bit me or not.' They pulled him in and saw that he had been bitten in half just below the heart."

Roger, shrinking against the side of the jeep, felt himself all over.

"Just want to make sure that I haven't been bitten in half," he said. "Why, that monster must have enough teeth for a dozen men."

"Enough for twenty-two men," Hal said. "A tiger shark has about 720 teeth—man has only 32. Of course I don't need to tell you that not all sharks are the same. Some have blunt teeth and seldom use them in fighting. The thresher shark fights with its tail and its bill, not its teeth. The whale shark has no teeth—it can't bite you, but it inhales you. The basking shark is one of the biggest of all, about forty feet, but is quite harmless. It feeds on tiny things no bigger than mosquitoes."

"I wish this thing would go away," Roger complained. "I'm getting tired of its company."

The tiger had no intention of going away. Instead, it gave a strong thrust of its tail and sent itself farther up into the glass shell. Now it might be able to reach either of the boys, although they had plastered themselves up as tightly as possible against the glass.

The shark twisted itself within reach of Roger. Its jaws were about to close on his shoulder when it gave a violent start and dropped out of the hole.

"What happened?" gasped Roger.

"Your dolphin came to the rescue. He rammed his hard head into the shark's tummy."

"Would a shark feel that?"

"Not if it struck his armor plate. But his underside is soft, and the dolphin knows it. Dolphins have often killed a shark by one blow where it hurts most."

But this shark was by no means dead, even though its small enemy had struck it harder than a mule can kick.

It wheeled about and went straight for Mr. Bottle. The terrific size of the creature made the boys fear for the dolphin's life. Nearly all marine animals of the Great Barrier Reef are larger than their cousins elsewhere. The tiger was a good thirty feet long. It must weigh at least seven tons, and the four-hundred-pound dolphin looked like a toy beside it.

The shark came on with amazing speed, maintaining its reputation as the fastest of all fish. In short bursts it could do fifty miles an hour.

The shark was not only the fastest and largest of fish, but the most dangerous. In that flashing moment Hal remembered what they had been told by one of the leading surgeons in Sydney. He had treated hundreds of cases of shark bite.

"It is possible," Dr. Coppleson had said, "that sharks in some other parts of the world are harmless, but in our waters they are certainly not. Here is a collection of over a hundred reports concerning men who have been attacked by sharks. As you can see, 80 percent of these cases were fatal. We have here in Australia five sorts of sharks that attack men: white sharks, tiger sharks, hammerheads, gray nurse sharks, and makos. As Australians, we are ashamed to have to say that Australia leads the world in shark attacks and deaths."

The boys would never forget the tiger's eyes as they looked at that moment. They were blacker than onyx, and powerful, calm, and cruel. No wonder that the English sea captain who in the sixteenth century had first placed one of these monsters on display in London named it from the German word *Schurke,* meaning villain. *Schurke* became "shark." It was still the villain of the sea.

The boys were astounded by the gape of those open jaws. Now they understood the Australian report that a great white had been cut open and the remains of a whole horse found inside. This was possible only because of the elastic muscles between the upper and lower jaws; they stretch like rubber bands so that the villain can take in food larger than its own head.

Before their eyes, they saw this happen. The cavern with its 720 terrible teeth took in Mr. Bottle's head and shoulders before he could get out a single whistle or click and proceeded to swallow him whole.

It was more than Roger could bear. Mr. Bottle had saved him, now he must save Mr. Bottle. Forgetting his own danger, deaf to the shout of warning from his brother, he plunged out of the glass jeep and made straight for the villain of the sea.

He had no idea yet what he would do. He had a knife in his belt, but he had sense enough to realize that he might as well attack this monster with a toothpick. He wished he had a spear gun—but that, too, would probably have been useless. He had no weapons but his bare hands.

He would try the dolphin's favorite trick. He swam beneath the shark, then came up with all the speed he could muster and rammed his hard head into the villain's tummy. The flesh went in like rubber but bounced out again like rubber. The shark didn't seem to mind in the least.

How about the gills? They were supposed to be very sensitive. Roger swam to the right gill and beat upon it with all the force of his fists.

The shark did not seem to feel it. It was too fully occupied in getting down its four-hundred-pound mouthful of food. This was a slow process, but very steady, and another inch of Roger's friend had now disappeared.

Roger could at least be glad that the shark had not bitten Mr. Bottle in two. There was no need to bite it if it could be swallowed whole. If the shark changed its mind and closed its teeth, that would be the end of Roger's dolphin. He must act fast, but what could he do?

He remembered that no fish liked to have anything on its back, whether it was octopus, giant squid, conger eel, or sea snake. Or man.

He swam up and came down straddling the back just behind the head.

This bothered him much more than it bothered the shark. Roger was not protected by a rubber suit but wore only a bathing suit, since these equatorial waters were very warm. The teeth that covered the tiger's back pierced his legs. Trickles of blood began to turn the water pink.

The tiger switched violently. It had caught the smell of blood, and that made it all the more determined to get this meal down as quickly as possible.

Through the pink mist Roger saw Hal coming to the rescue. Roger wanted to win this battle all by himself. What could his brother do? Nothing more than he could.

There was one thing he had not tried. He had battered the belly and punched the gill and tried to distract the creature by straddling its back.

But those great black eyes. They were more tender than stomach, gills, or back. Roger leaned forward and sank his thumbs into the two black pools.

The shark took notice of him for the first time. It thrashed about violently, churning up the water, frightening away the reef fish. It took to swimming around in a circle, its tail beating violently while the tortured dolphin's tail beat as violently in front. Here was something new in natural history —a monster with a tail at each end.

Roger was nearly unhorsed by the frenzied creature's leaps and surges. He must not lose his grip and fall off. He pressed his bare legs more tightly against the cruel teeth, regardless of the pain, and dug his thumbs deeper into the eyes. His mount was now circling at such speed that Hal was left hopelessly behind.

Roger could see that his strategy was having some effect. The shark was loosening its hold on the dolphin. Roger had spoiled its appetite. Now it could only think of escaping those cruel thumbs.

Mr. Bottle evidently thought that at last there was some hope of escape, and wriggled more vigorously. The teeth no longer held him, but still he could not pull loose. The muscles of the great fish's throat held him fast. How could Roger help free him from these great rubbery pincers that gripped his head?

The boy decided it was time for the last act. He leaned forward with the idea of helping the dolphin to pry himself loose, but could not reach him. He saw that he did not need to put his thumbs back into the shark's eyes; the pain he had already inflicted was enough. Enough to make the shark forget its meal, but not enough to rescue the dolphin.

If he could only get hold of the dolphin's tail and pull him free. Suddenly it occurred to him—there was a way to do that.

He slid off the shark's back, scraping himself more badly in the process. He turned about and got ready to meet the shark as it came round again. He saw that Hal had done the same thing. Between them they might be able to lay hold of that squirming black tail that projected from the shark's mouth like the tongue of a great snake.

Here it came, the weird double animal. The shark's bleary

eyes did not see the two obstacles that lay ahead until within a dozen feet of them. One obstacle was big and the other only half its size. With a strong thrust of its tail the shark avoided the big thing and came within reach of the smaller one.

Roger grabbed the waving tail of the dolphin.

It was then that the shark made a serious mistake. It wrenched to one side to avoid the strange object that it dimly saw blocking its path. Thus it did what Roger could not have done by himself. With Roger holding firmly to the tail, the sidelong twist was enough to jerk the dolphin loose from the grip of those powerful throat muscles.

Out came Mr. Bottle, so dazed by his experience that he lay without movement like a dead thing. For a moment Roger feared that he really was dead. Trapped in the shark's throat, he had been unable to get to the surface to breathe. Perhaps he had suffocated.

Roger must get that blowhole into the air at once. The air mixture inside the glass jeep would do. Hal came to help. One on each side, locking their arms around their helpless friend, they propelled him toward the jeep. The effort to move this inert dead weight of four hundred pounds made them breathe heavily from their scuba tanks, but at last they crawled up into the jeep and drew the animal's head above water.

Hal put his hand close to the blowhole. His face became very grave.

"Well," said Roger anxiously, "is he breathing or not?"

"He is not," Hal said. "I'll try artificial respiration."

But how do you practice mouth-to-mouth resuscitation with a dolphin? In this case it must be mouth-to-blowhole.

Hal placed his mouth over the blowhole and exhaled, inhaled, exhaled, inhaled.

He kept this up until he was blue in the face. It takes a lot of air to fill and empty the lungs of a dolphin.

Roger pushed him aside and took his place.

Hal put his ear to the dolphin's chest. "His heart is still beating. Keep it up—I think he'll come around."

Roger kept it up until he was completely winded.

He stopped to rest, while keeping his face close to the blowhole. He felt a breeze fanning his cheek. It came and went. He suddenly realized it was no breeze.

"He's breathing!" he exclaimed.

The dolphin's soft brown eyes were fixed upon him. A weak smile curved the animal's lips. Mr. Bottle seemed to know to whom he owed his new lease on life. He clicked a little. It was a very faint click, more like the chirp of a small bird.

Roger and Hal still supported him. Roger stroked his neck. The animal's strength rapidly came back. Soon he was whistling and clicking like mad, saying a hundred thank-yous in his own two languages.

He began to struggle a little, and the boys let him go. He dropped out of the hatch and swam happily about.

A voice came over the radiotelephone. "Captain Murphy calling Hal Hunt."

Hal replied, "This is Hunt. Where are you, Captain?"

"Over your head," replied the captain.

"It must be the *Flying Cloud*," cried Roger.

This was to be their own ship for a while. They had chartered it in Sydney and had left it in the shipyard to be fitted with tanks to hold the fish and other sea animals they hoped to capture to send home to their father's aquarium on Long Island. It would carry their prizes to Sydney where they would be transshipped on cargo vessels to America.

They had named it *Flying Cloud* because of its glorious white cloud of sails.

The Good Ship Flying Cloud

"Let's go aboard the *Flying Cloud,*" Roger said excitedly. "I'll start the motor."

"No, wait," said Hal. "First we'd better talk about this a bit. We can't go aboard."

"Why not?"

"We might get the bends."

Roger objected, "You're off your head. You get the bends when you've been breathing ordinary air. We've been breathing helium."

"You're right—and wrong," said Hal. "It's true that you have more trouble if you've been breathing air, because air is 80 percent nitrogen. If you don't come up very slowly and give your lungs time to get rid of the nitrogen, it makes bubbles in your blood that cause cramps in your muscles and joints, and that's what they call the bends. The helium mixture that you've been breathing has only a small amount of oxygen and nitrogen, so you're not so likely to get a bad case of the bends. But still you have to be careful. I'll tell you what we can do. We can go up until the top of the jeep is just above the surface. Then we can get a good look at our ship. But we'll stay there only a minute and come right down. Now you can start the motor."

Roger looked at the dolphin, swimming round and round the jeep. "I just had a better idea. Let's go without the motor."

"How can you do that?"

"Let Bottle take us. He can be a big help to us if we train him right. Now's a good chance to begin."

He slipped out of the jeep and stopped the circling dolphin which clicked and clattered affectionately and rubbed itself against him much as a cat rubs itself against the legs of a friendly human.

Roger took the end of the towrope attached to the nose of the jeep and placed it in the dolphin's mouth. Then, with his hand still on the rope, he started to swim toward the *Flying Cloud*, gently drawing the dolphin along with him.

Once the dolphin separated its jaws and the line dropped out. Roger replaced it and pinched the jaws together to give his friend the idea that he must hold the line tight. The boy guided the dolphin close to the ship where a rope ladder dangled to the water.

A sailor who had seen the operation came down and took the end of the line.

The dolphin had learned its first lesson. Hal understood what Roger was trying to do. He wanted to make Bottle a good messenger between Undersea City and the *Flying Cloud*. The boys themselves, though breathing mostly helium with only a trace of nitrogen, could not go up and down without some danger of getting the bends, but the dolphin had no such difficulty. Dolphins could and did swim up and down between the surface and depths of a thousand feet or more without the least trouble. They were ideal delivery boys. A famous dolphin, Tuffy, made a name for itself as an expert messenger carrying mail, tools, and supplies between the surface ship and Sea Lab II, two hundred feet down.

With the top of the glass jeep above water, the boys could plainly see their ship and the captain looking over the rail. They had met him and his two-man crew in Sydney, where they had chartered the ship.

Captain Ted Murphy was a genial man with a leathery face, tanned by the tropic sun and wrinkled by smiles and rough weather.

The *Flying Cloud* was Captain Ted's own ship, but it belonged to the boys as long as they held their charter. And they were very proud of it. From bowsprit to rudder it measured eighty feet and had a beam of thirty. It was equipped with an auxiliary engine but depended chiefly upon its magnificent spread of sail. Its engine served only to get it in and out between the reefs. Given a fair wind, its sails would carry it along at seventeen knots. Indeed it had formerly been used as a racing yacht and had won several of the annual cup races.

Hal had ordered the construction of specimen tanks, and the captain now assured him that they had been built—two large tanks for the large fish, and several small ones so that creatures who were inclined to eat each other could be kept apart. All the tanks had lids that could be left off in fair weather but clamped shut in rough weather so that fish and water could not splash out.

Hal congratulated the captain on a good job, then powered the jeep down. Roger was feeling his right shoulder.

"What's the matter, kid?" Hal asked.

"Nothing," Roger said.

"When you say nothing, it's something. Your shoulder hurts—right? We'll go deeper."

When the depth gauge registered nearly two hundred feet, Roger showed relief. "Pain's gone," he said.

"Good," said Hal. "That was a near one. It just shows that we can't risk running up and down."

"Then how'll we ever get out?"

"When we get ready to come out permanently, we will have to come up very, very slowly to allow plenty of time to get rid of the nitrogen. A real case of the bends could paralyze a man for life. Remember that poor old fellow we saw in a wheelchair in the Hawaiian Islands? He had been diving off the coast of Lahaina to get black coral which grows only at great depths. That was forty years ago. He's been in a wheelchair ever since. He was lucky. Other black-coral divers have died as soon as they got to the surface."

The dolphin faithfully followed them down. They parked the glass bug in the garage and crawled up into their cottage. Bottle stuck his head up through the hole and started a conversation.

"It's nice to get down again," said Roger. "Boy, wasn't it hot up there? Must have been over a hundred degrees." He looked at a thermometer on the wall. "Here it's only seventy-five."

"Yes," Hal said. "There's a lot to be said for undersea climate. It's really better than the climate topside. People who live beneath the sea will not be bothered by typhoons, cyclones, tornadoes and hurricanes, thunder and lightning. There will be no snowstorms or hailstorms, no sand and dust storms like those that plague the American West. No smog. No flood will wash away an underwater town, no fire can burn homes that are insulated by water. No noise except the croaks of croaker fish, grunts of groupers, and other small sounds. It's been called the silent world. It's not silent, but its sounds are nothing compared with the roar of cars, trucks, trains, and planes.

"There are plenty of difficulties and dangers down here, but bad weather and noise are not among them. The temperature, which goes popping up and down on land, is not so wobbly beneath the sea. It stays about the same, day and night, week after week, year after year.

"You do have to watch out for sea animals that bite, scratch, or sting, but wounds generally heal almost overnight. Cousteau found that out in his village under the Red Sea. On the ship up above, in the burning heat, ordinary cuts took as much as three weeks to heal. Below, the same wounds disappeared in two days. Something to do with the difference in bacteria. The men up above steadily lost weight. The men below stayed rosy and plump. There's a chance that the future people who live out their lives beneath the sea will live longer, perhaps well over a hundred."

Bottle was bouncing up and down, eager to play, work, do something.

"I'll give you something to do," Roger said.

He wrote on a piece of paper, *Just to see if it works.*

He put it in a plastic bag, tied the bag shut with cord, and put the end of the cord between the dolphin's teeth.

Would the dolphin remember the last time a rope was put in his mouth?

At once Bottle dropped out of the hole, swam swiftly upward and out of sight.

In only two or three minutes he was back, the bag still hanging from his mouth. Roger was disappointed. "There hasn't been time for him to get up to the ship and back. I guess he's not as bright as I thought."

He took the bag and opened it. "Yes, my note is still there. You dumb dolphin! A fine message boy you are."

Idly, he unfolded the paper. Then he gave an excited yelp. Under his note the captain had written, *It works.*

Roger stroked the wet head of the dolphin. "I beg your pardon for saying you were dumb. You're as smart as they come. And how speedy!"

Swift delivery between sea bottom and ship was now possible. It was no small victory, and Hal was as pleased as Roger. But the most pleased seemed to be the dolphin. He whistled with pride and pleasure. But at this moment something or someone gave him a violent jab and he disappeared.

A face by no means so pleasant as the dolphin's came up through the hole.

Rascal or Saint?

Kaggs stared at the boys.

"Well, I'll be a donkey's uncle," he growled. "They told me somebody would be coming in, but I didn't know it would be you."

"Nice of you to remember us," Hal said.

"I thought you were dead," Kaggs grumbled.

"You did your best to make sure we'd be dead," said Hal. "Last time we saw you was when you sailed away and left us to die on a desert island."

Kaggs smiled an evil smile. "Well, now, that was just a little fun. Anyhow that's all past and gone." He tried to be a little more agreeable. "I'm sure you're not the sort to hold a grudge against anybody. There's no reason we can't be friends."

He climbed in and went to his room to take off his gear and get into dry clothes.

He came back and sat down. "Now, boys, I think we should have a little talk. Did the boss tell you I was here?"

"He did."

"Did you say you had met me before?"

"Yes."

"Are you going to tell him anything about—about what went on?"

"We can't promise," Hal said.

Kaggs's face darkened. "So, you can't promise. Well, you'd better promise. I belong here. You know I used to be a pearl trader in these islands."

"Or a pearl stealer," Hal said. "And now you think you have a good thing going here. The stealing should be good where men will be digging up gold and silver and perhaps diamonds and pearls and treasure from wrecks and rare specimens of animal life that will be worth thousands of dollars . . ."

"Now, now," Kaggs interrupted. "You have me all wrong. I know I didn't behave myself very well when you knew me. But all that is changed. I pretended to be a man of the Bible. Now I really am. I saw the error of my ways. I was a crook. You see I own up to it frankly. I went around under an assumed name, the Reverend Archibald Jones. I didn't tell anybody I had done two murders and spent a spell in prison. All that is behind me. I am here under my own name, Merlin Kaggs. That ought to be enough to convince you that I have changed. Now I think only of others—not of myself. Don't you think I deserve another chance? If you peach on me I am ruined. I want you to promise to keep mum."

"Don't you think you are asking too much? We should tell all we know about you so as to protect Dr. Dick and people here against any more of your dirty work."

"But I tell you I've changed," protested Kaggs. "I've returned to my mother's knee. In memory of my saintly father —he was a clergyman, you know—I only want to do good from now on."

"Horsefeathers!" Roger exploded.

Kaggs looked at him severely. "Young fellow, that's no

way to speak to a man of the Lord. I shall pray for you both."

He went to his room.

"I vote we tell Dr. Dick all about him," Roger said.

His older brother shook his head. "I don't like to do that. There's just one chance in a thousand that he means what he says. Perhaps it's only one chance in a million—I don't know. Anyhow, there's no rush. Let's wait and see how things go."

"I'm afraid they'll go from bad to worse," his brother said. "Oh, I know how you feel—you've got the crazy idea that there's some good in everybody. That's because you've had too much to do with animals. There's some good in any animal, but I'm not so sure about people. Especially Kaggs. I'm afraid of him. If we don't promise to be quiet, he'll try to do us in."

"That's a bridge we'll cross when we come to it," Hal said.

Hal was soon much too busy to worry about Kaggs. He had a hundred ideas. He boiled with ambition to put them into practice.

"First," he told Dr. Dick, "I'd like to go fishing."

Dr. Dick's eyebrows went up. This young naturalist had been engaged to do some very serious work. And right at the start he wanted to play hooky and go fishing.

Hal grinned. "I know what you're thinking. But I'm not really a playboy. In fact, I think fishing is about the most important thing I can do. Millions of people are on the edge of starvation. But there are billions upon billions of good food fish in the sea. Our fishermen don't get them. Oh, they let down a hook and pull up one fish, or a net and pull up a few dozen. Our ancestors did the same thing a thousand years ago. Fishing methods haven't kept up with the times."

"I agree with you," Dr. Dick said. "Do you think you can spark a revolution in fishing?"

"I don't know. But I'd surely like to try. I've been thinking about it a lot. In New York before we came I bought modern equipment that should make it possible to bring up thousands of fish at a time instead of one or a hundred."

"What sort of equipment?"

"Slurp guns, stiletto lights, machines for fishing by electric shock, ultrasonic beam instruments, anesthetics, milking machines to milk whales, laser beam units, and an airlift like a vacuum cleaner to pump whole schools of fish up into a ship."

Dr. Dick was looking at Hal as if he had never seen him before. "I think we got more than we bargained for when we got you. Most of those things are new to me. Some of them I have heard of, but never dreamed they could be used for fishing."

"Perhaps they can't," admitted Hal. "That's what we will find out."

"They sound expensive," said Dr. Dick. "I think the foundation should pay for them. If you give me a bill I will see that it is paid."

"There will be no bill," Hal said. "Let's say they are the contribution of John Hunt and Sons to your project. After all, we don't know whether they will work or not."

"One question," Dr. Dick said. "Many fish are no good as food. How are you going to find great schools of good food fish that you can bring up by the thousands?"

"One way," said Hal, "will be to let our friend help us."

"Who is that? Kaggs?"

"No, not Kaggs. Our new friend is the gentleman who is looking in through the window. Dr. Dick, meet Mr. Bottle."

The scientist stared at the dolphin. "Why, that's just a dolphin—how can it help you?"

"Sonar," Hal said.

Dr. Dick shook his head. "I don't understand you. But I have a lot of faith in you. Go ahead with your experiments, and good luck to you."

Hal and Roger took off again in the jeep and Bottle followed. This time Roger handled the stick expertly and he gave the windows of the next house a wide berth and ran no danger of nipping off the heads of walkers and swimmers in Barracuda Street.

"What are we looking for?" Roger asked.

"A big school of fish."

"But there are fish all around us."

"Yes, but most of them aren't good to eat. Just now we're interested only in fish that would make good food."

It was a long search before they found what they were after —a large school of fat fish all close together and pointed in the same direction like birds on migration.

"Just the thing," Hal said. "Tuna—fine eating. It has taken us more than an hour to find them. But it takes a surface ship days to locate a school of tuna. And then each fisherman pulls out one at a time on hook and line. All that makes tuna in the stores cost ten times what it would cost if the schools could be found quickly and easily and the fish could be drawn up by thousands instead of by ones. A lot of people around the world who can't afford to buy tuna or any other flesh could then buy it. I'll leave you for a little while."

He dropped out of the jeep, swam to the dolphin, petted him, then put his arm around his neck and swam with him to the school of tuna.

The tuna, as curious as most fish, gathered around the man and the dolphin. Bottle tried to grab one of them but Hal restrained him. He must not be allowed to frighten the fish by attacking them. He stayed for many minutes to give Bottle plenty of time to get it through his head that these fish were something special, something more important to his human friend than most fish.

When Hal thought there had been time for this lesson to sink in, he took Bottle back to the jeep.

He stayed a few minutes, then turned his companion around and set off again toward the school. Since the tuna had been swimming slowly, they were not exactly where they had been before. This time Hal let Bottle act as the guide. The dolphin immediately set off toward the new location of the school. He didn't wait to be led—he towed his friend along so fast that Hal need do no swimming but simply hang on. Again they visited the school, and again returned to the jeep. They all went back to the house but did not park the jeep in the garage.

After ten minutes in the house, Hal said, "Now we will see what he has learned. You get into the jeep ready to go. I'll be with you in a minute."

He slipped out and again put his arm around Bottle's neck. He began to take Bottle where the school was—or had been.

But Bottle would have none of it. He struck off in a different direction. Hal let him go, climbed into the jeep, and followed him.

"It's no good," Roger said. "He's going in the wrong direction. He doesn't know what you want him to do."

"We'll see," Hal said. "Perhaps he knows what he's doing. Put on more power. He's shooting along like a torpedo."

The dolphin constantly clicked as it swam. "What's all the clicking for?" Roger wondered.

"Sonar," Hal said. Before he could explain, they sighted the school of tuna.

Before, it had taken them one hour to find the school. Now they had reached it in two minutes.

Roger was puzzled. "Why didn't he go where the school had been. Instead he took an entirely new direction."

"Sonar is the answer," Hal said. "Sonar is a way to use echoes. You know how a bat can fly around in complete darkness and avoid bumping into rocks, trees, or anything else. It keeps making little noises that bounce back from anything they strike. The bat steers itself by these echoes. It can tell just how near it is to the object by the strength of the echo. The dolphin can do the same thing. That's why he keeps clicking—so he can guide himself by the echoes. And that's why he took a new direction. The school had been swimming and wasn't where it had been."

Roger objected, "But there must have been thousands of echoes coming from all around. How could he tell which echo came from the school of tuna?"

Hal shook his head. "Now you've asked the million-dollar question. Nobody knows—yet. The American Navy is spending a million dollars a year trying to find out."

"Why is it so important?"

"Because if we knew just how the dolphin's echo system works, we could make a machine to do the same thing. That may take many years. In the meantime they have learned some amazing things about the dolphin. One of their researchers, Dr. Winthrop Kellogg, has found that the dolphin doesn't even need to see to find what he is after. Dr. Kellogg blindfolded a dolphin and then threw a fish into the water. The dolphin went straight for the fish and swallowed it."

"That's hard to believe," Roger said.

"So it is. But here's something harder to believe. Kellogg proved that a blindfolded dolphin can tell the difference between one kind of fish and another. A certain dolphin liked mullet but hated sprats. He was blindfolded and put in a tank with both. He promptly went around the sprats and gobbled down the mullets.

"The dolphin, with its eyes still covered, was put in a tank with one mullet and one imitation mullet made of plastic. It was exactly the same size and shape as the real mullet. The dolphin gave it the cold shoulder and went straight for the real fish.

"Another dolphin was taught to play a sort of game of ball.

The dolphin was shown a steel ball and at the same time he was given a fish. Then he was introduced to another steel ball just a tiny bit smaller and he got no fish. Then he was blindfolded and both balls were thrown into the water. He immediately shot down and brought up the larger ball and was given a fish. He repeated this performance twenty times without a single mistake. And there was so little difference in the size of the balls that the trainer couldn't tell them apart and had to use calipers to find out which was larger. But the dolphin's sonar took him to the right ball every time."

Roger looked at his dolphin with pride. "Golly, he's smarter than we are."

Hal agreed. "In some ways, much smarter."

"But there's one thing I don't understand," said Roger. "You've proved that a dolphin can find in a few seconds a school of fish that it might take a fishing smack many hours or even days to locate. But after you've found your fish, how do you get them up into the boat?"

"Good question," Hal said. "We'll try to find an answer right now. Hand me that radiophone."

He took the instrument and called, *"Flying Cloud*, Captain Ted Murphy, are you there? Captain Ted, *Glass Jeep* calling."

After a moment came the reply, "Murphy speaking. Is this Hal Hunt?"

"Right. Ted, we're going to send up some fish. Fill the big tank. We'll come near you and let up a signal buoy at the end of a line. Follow the flag and we'll guide you to the fish. Make ready to drop the vac."

"Got it," replied Captain Ted. "Okay and out."

"What's the vac?" Roger asked.

"The vacuum cleaner. You know—the big suction hose we bought in New York."

Roger looked puzzled. But he asked no more questions. He would just wait and see.

The jeep, aided by Bottle, led the ship to a point directly above the great school of tuna.

"All right, Ted. Let 'er down, and turn on the pump."

The great black hose snaked down. "Turn on the searchlight," Hal said. For centuries fishermen had known that a bright light attracts fish. Roger switched on the light. The tuna at once gathered near it.

Hal slipped out of the jeep and took the end of the hose. It was trembling with the powerful pull of the pump. Hal was careful not to put his arm near the nozzle. That was a good way to lose an arm. The suction was so great that it had been known to draw the blood out through a man's skin.

The vac was nothing new. It had been used for years by treasure hunters to suck up the sand that covered old wrecks. But no one had thought to use it for fish. That was Hal's idea, and he had no notion whether it would work or not.

Fish shot into the hose faster than he could count them. He directed the nozzle wherever the fish were thickest. Up they streamed, and into the tank above. Dozens, scores, hundreds, made the climb within minutes. Their place was taken by other fish, crowding in toward the light, curious about this great black snake. They were swallowed by it before they could flip a tail. Within ten minutes the entire school numbering several thousand fish had gone aboard the *Flying Cloud*. A fishing smack would require days, perhaps even weeks, to equal this record.

Hal returned to the jeep and took up the phone. "That's it, Ted."

"Heavens to Betsy," came back the voice of the astonished captain. "The fish in that tank are packed together like sardines."

"Good," Hal said. "Take them in to Cairns and deliver them to the fishing co-op. And tell them how we got them."

Hal went to report to Dr. Dick. Dick listened with wide-eyed astonishment.

"Never heard anything like it in my life," he said. "Do you know, young man, that you've just started a revolution in fishing? Fishing by dolphin and vacuum cleaner! I'm going to send the story in to the scientific journals and the Associated Press. The AP will syndicate it to newspapers all over the world. There'll come a day when every fisherman will begin to think in terms of dolphin and vac instead of hook and net. But will the supply of tuna hold out?"

"It's not limited to tuna," Hal said. "There are lots of other good food fish that travel in schools—albacore, mullet, bass, cod, menhaden, barracuda, cobia, kingfish, wahoo, dorado, and a hundred others. Of course my scheme falls flat when it comes to fish that don't school and are too big to go up a vac—swordfish, sawfish, shark, Pacific sea bass, and so on. I'm thinking about other ways to get them."

"You have a good think-machine," Dr. Dick said. "I'm sure you will solve that problem, too."

Killer Whale

"We have visitors," Roger said when Hal returned to the cottage. "There they are, just outside."

Two other dolphins had joined Bottle. Now they came and thrust their heads up through the "front door" in the floor. All three sent up fountains of spray from their blowholes as dolphins and porpoises commonly do when they thrust their heads into air.

Kaggs happened to be sitting near by and got the full benefit of the shower. He leaped up, wiped his face, and said angrily, "That's the limit. I object to sharing this cottage with three wild beasts." He kicked at the nearest one, and all three dropped out of the hole.

Roger was annoyed. "That's no way to treat guests."

Kaggs growled, "They're no guests of mine. If you want to associate with animals, that's your lookout. Perhaps you're half animal yourselves. I'm above that sort of thing."

"I'm sorry they frightened you," Roger said.

"Frightened nothing," Kaggs retorted. "It would take more than that to scare me."

He promptly got more than that. He got the shock of his life.

Up through the hole came two terrific jaws. They towered up into the room five feet high. Both upper and lower jaws bristled with savage teeth. There were half a hundred teeth and each was as long as a man's hand and sharp as a spear. The great mouth looked like that of a huge crocodile.

The monster gnashed these great teeth together with a sound like that of a machine gun. The terrified Kaggs shrank into the farthest corner of the room.

"It's a killer whale," Hal said.

That was enough for Kaggs. He slid along the wall to the door of his own room, got inside, and slammed the door.

Here was a creature that had often been described as the "most fearful animal on land or sea." There were many stories of killers having bitten holes in small boats, upset the occupants, and swallowed them whole. And yet, whenever these stories had been carefully investigated, it was found that the attacks had been made by great sharks and not by killer whales.

"What do you suppose made him come around?" said Roger.

Hal said, "I suppose he saw the dolphins visiting us and he wanted to take a look, too. He belongs to the dolphin family, you know—he's the biggest of all the dolphins. He's the fastest of them all and the most dangerous to other animals. Those jaws can bite a sea lion in two with one snap. He is not afraid of the largest whale. He will attack it, tear at its lips, get inside its mouth, and devour its tongue—that's the bit of food he likes best.

"He has a stomach six feet long. In the stomach of one dead killer, men found fourteen seals and thirteen dolphins. They had all been swallowed whole."

"But why would he attack dolphins? You said he belongs to the family."

"He does. But men attack men, don't they, and why shouldn't a great dolphin attack smaller ones?"

"But he didn't do anything to those three dolphins who had their heads in the hole. He just pushed them out of the way."

"I don't know why," Hal said. "Perhaps he thought they were going to attack us."

"What would he care if they did?"

"He's like the other dolphins," Hal said. "He's the friend of man. Oh, I know there have been plenty of tales about him attacking men, but it's my personal opinion that they are all nonsense. And I don't believe he has any desire to bite holes in boats. It's not that he couldn't do it. He could very easily. His teeth could go through a hull two inches thick. The thinnest hulls on all the oceans are the hulls of the Eskimo kayaks. They're made of sealskins less than a quarter inch thick, but there isn't a single reliable record of a skin boat being attacked by a killer whale."

"Do you think I could make a pet of him?" Roger wondered.

Hal laughed. "A pretty big pet. He must be thirty feet long and weighs as much as an elephant. But I believe you could do it. It has been done. At that oceanarium near San Diego called Sea World they have a pet killer whale named Shamu. He comes whenever you call him, carries articles here and there, draws a canoe by a loop over his head, tows a man hanging on to a fin, rings a bell, walks on his tail, leaps clear up out of the water, and even sings a song—though I wouldn't say he is a very good opera star. He lets men ride on his back round and round the pool at a terrific pace. He opens his mouth to have his great razor-sharp teeth brushed by a giant toothbrush. He actually lets his trainer put his head into his mouth."

"Do you think this one would let me do that?" Roger asked.

"I don't know. I wouldn't like to see you try it."

The killer whale was talking. "I think he's asking me to come and do it," Roger said.

Hal objected, "You're letting your imagination run away with you. I don't want a brother without any head."

Roger moved closer to the great mouth. The sight of it gave him a chilly feeling down his backbone. The jaws were as tall as he was.

Roger talked as quietly as he would have spoken to a kitten. He kept this up for many minutes, moving a little closer all the time. The great jaws stood open as if waiting for something juicy to fall into them.

Roger wished he hadn't begun this experiment. Hot and cold waves seemed to be running over his body. But he couldn't stop now. He wouldn't let his brother see that he was scared out of his wits. Nor could he let the animal know that he was frightened. That would only make him more likely to attack. If he really wanted to make the monster his pal, he must go through with this.

Finally he stood close enough to touch the visitor. He did a little more soft talking, then gingerly reached out and stroked the smooth hide just under the chin. Cats, dogs, and dolphins liked this, perhaps killer whales did, too.

"That's enough for now," Hal said. "Wait till later to do the rest."

"I think he's in the mood right now," Roger said.

He brought his hand up and stroked the lip. Then, still speaking quietly, he put his hand up over the sharp teeth.

Down came the upper jaw. The hand was lightly gripped between the upper and lower teeth.

It was a test, and Roger knew it. He had enough knowledge of animals to know that if he snatched away his hand now, his chance to become friend and trainer of this animal was gone. The points of the sharp teeth were not too comfortable. Those teeth could go through his hand like a knife through butter.

The teeth relaxed their hold. Now Roger could withdraw his hand. Instead, he reached farther in until his arm was in up to the elbow. Hal held his breath.

The killer was talking back, and although Roger did not understand his language, he felt that the tone was friendly. He slowly took out his hand and scratched the whale again under the chin. Then he brought his face close and looked down the monster's throat. It was big enough to swallow him at one gulp.

Roger rather expected to feel the hot breath of the creature on his face. But no air was stirring. Then he remembered that the breathing was done through the blowhole, not through the mouth. There was no smell from the mouth. A crocodile's mouth stank, because bits of the meat it had eaten remained between the teeth. But the killer whale did not chew his food —he swallowed everything whole. The teeth were for hanging on to wriggling fish, not chewing them. The teeth were all canines for gripping, no molars for grinding.

Roger very slowly put his face between the open jaws. It was like going into a cave. There was plenty of room for half a dozen heads like his.

He brought his entire head within the two rows of teeth. Now if the jaws closed on his neck, he would be trapped and nothing could pull him loose. He was glad his mother couldn't see him now—she would faint.

Brave and Almost Brainy

Roger slowly withdrew his head from the jaws of death. He couldn't help heaving a deep sigh of relief.

His brother also was very happy to have the experiment over with. "Thank goodness," he said, "he could tell the difference between your head and a fish. He must be very intelligent."

"How about that?" Roger asked. "Is he really very intelligent? I always thought the elephant was about the most brainy of the animals."

"The killer whale's brain is about seven times as large as the elephant's," Hal said. "People who know the land but don't know the sea imagine that the elephant and the chimpanzee are the most intelligent of the nonhumans. But experiments with the dolphins, including the killer, show that they have a higher IQ than any other animal we know about in the sea or on the land.

"A great trainer named Frohn who used to put on animal shows said about the dolphins: 'Of all the animals I've worked with, these are the ones who catch on quickest to what you want them to do.' You've seen the dolphin Flipper on TV. His trainer is O. Feldman, and he says, 'As soon as I can get him to understand some new trick I want him to do, he does it, and he'll never forget. Six months later I can give him the same signal, maybe no more than a click of my fingers, and he'll do exactly the same thing.'

"The famous scientist Dr. Lilly, who has made the study of dolphins his life work, goes even further. He says dolphins learn as fast as humans. The killer whale knows the difference between a steamer and a sailing ship. If he is chased by a steamer, he goes deep to escape it. If he is chased by a ship under sail, he knows that all he has to do is to go straight into the wind and the ship can't follow him.

"And killers have their own language. If one is attacked, he can warn other members of the herd. The alarm can be sent instantly as far as six or seven miles away. If one is wounded by a harpoon gun, the kind that a whaling ship carries on its bow, he warns others to look out for harpoon guns, and to make them understand, he must be able to describe the weapon so that they will recognize it when they see it."

"If he's so smart, he should be able to help us a lot," Roger said. "But what can he do that a dolphin can't do?"

"Well, for one thing, he can pull heavier loads than any dolphin. He can easily tow a ton. He has the strength of a team of elephants. The dolphins can run many of our errands up to the ship and back carrying tools and loads of fish, but when it's something very heavy it will be a good job for the killer whale. The only question is whether we can get him to stick around."

"I think he'll stay with us," said Roger.

"I don't know," Hal said. "He's gone already."

Sure enough, the "front door" was empty. Roger anxiously looked out the window. There he saw his new friend swimming about close-by. Up and down Barracuda Street swam the killer whale, and terrified people rushed to get into their houses. They knew a killer whale when they saw one by its dorsal fin six feet high, its black back and white belly, and terrible jaws, and they had read the wild stories of this evil creature said to be the most fearful animal on land or sea.

But Hal and Roger and the other experimenters knew better. If everybody knew, perhaps the senseless murder of killer whales would stop.

Hal called up Dr. Dick and reported what had happened.

"You've made an important contribution to science," Dr. Dick said. "Your brother had a lot of courage—and brains."

"Yes," agreed Hal, "I think he's brave and even a bit brainy."

He saw that Roger was listening, so he added mischievously, "almost as brainy as a killer whale."

The door of Kaggs's room slowly opened and Kaggs peered out. When he saw that the great jaws were gone, he threw out his chest like a pouter pigeon and came in.

"Why didn't you stay to see the show?" Hal asked. "Were you afraid of our visitor?"

"Well—I—no, of course not—but I have more important things to do than to watch a stupid animal."

Roger resented the remark. He said, "If you think that killer whale is stupid, you are pretty stupid yourself."

Kaggs glared at the boy as if he could shrivel him with a look. He opened his mouth to make an angry reply, then seemed to think better of it. After a moment he replied softly:

"There was a time when I would have flayed you alive for that. But now that I have made my peace with the Lord, all I want is peace on earth. And under the sea. As I said in my sermon last Sunday, much of man's destiny in the future will be lived out in this world beneath the waves—a world four times as great as the dry world above. Until now this has been a world of peace. But the troubles that infest that old world begin to threaten the new. The Great Powers are rivals for possession of the ocean floor. Russia's underocean fleet is twice the size of Britain's and America's combined. America is arming her Polaris subs to be ready in case of war. We must avoid wars in the depths. And the way to insure brotherhood between the nations is to begin with brotherhood between man and man, between ourselves right here in Undersea City, in every home. And that means between you and me."

He enveloped both boys in a great smile that seemed strange on the cruel face they had known in the past.

"A very good sermon," Hal said.

Even Roger was touched. "I'm sorry I said what I did."

Kaggs's smile broadened. "That's all right, my boy. In this quiet undersea world I am sure we'll all find it easy to forgive and forget." He retired to his room.

Hal and Roger were silent for a few moments. Then Hal said, "Maybe he was sincere. What do you think?"

"I don't know what to think," said Roger.

The three young naturalists, Hal, Roger, and Bottle, had solved the problem of taking up a whole school of hundreds of fish and pouring them into a ship, thus doing in a few minutes what would have taken many days to accomplish by the old methods.

That would work well with small and even medium-size fish. But how about the great ones, too large to go up a vacuum hose? The saw of the sawfish would not fit in any hose, the marlin's spear would puncture the vac. The wahoo was a whopper, the grouper and the giant barracuda grew to immense size, and some sharks were as big as telephone booths. Yes, and how about the whale?

"To get the big fish," Hal said, "there are a couple of experiments I'd like to make."

He went to the phone and called up Captain Ted.

"Ted, I'm going to send up Bottle. Give him the electro fishing outfit and the laser machine. I'm going to see if I can use them to hunt down the big ones."

"Very well," replied Captain Ted. "But I don't see how you can fish with those things. And I've spent fifty years at sea."

"You spent the last fifty years," Hal said. "The next fifty years may be different. Of course these things may not work, but I'd like to try them out. Oh, yes, another thing I'd like to have—one of those packages of balloons and a bottle of compressed air."

Captain Ted laughed. "Now that's one for the book. Fishing by balloon! You're sure the helium hasn't gone to your head?"

"Perhaps it has," Hal admitted. "Anyhow, watch for Bottle."

"Will do," Ted replied, and Hal could hear him chuckling again as he rang off.

Bottle, as usual, was waiting and ready with his head poked up through the front door. Hal put a short length of rope into the dolphin's mouth. Bottle had learned by this time that this meant a trip up to the *Flying Cloud*. But Hal didn't want to do this rope trick every time Bottle was sent on an errand. So he pointed up, and at the same time looked up, and said very distinctly, "Ship—ship—ship." Other trainers had taught dolphins to obey spoken commands. Perhaps he could do the same. Again he repeated several times the word "ship."

From the dolphin's blowhole came an answer. This time it

was not a click or a whistle but an imitation of Hal's voice. It was not a very good imitation, but certainly the animal was trying to say "ship." He ducked out of the hole and shot upward. Immediately the other two dolphins and the killer whale followed him.

"Good," exclaimed Hal, much pleased. "I was *hoping* that Big Boy would go along. That will teach him where to go when we send him on an errand."

In less than five minutes Bottle was back. Captain Ted had put a loop around his neck and to the loop was attached a net containing the articles Hal had ordered.

That was not all Bottle had brought with him. In addition to Big Boy and the two dolphins there were now half a dozen more dolphins. Dolphins love company, and they are very curious. These new recruits had evidently been interested in Bottle and his friends, the ship above, and Bottle's load of instruments, and now they were fascinated by the humans in the house below. They swam round and round the house, looking in the windows, poking their heads up the "front door," keeping up a continuous whistling and clicking. Hal was delighted.

"This is too good to be true," he said. "The more who join the gang, the better."

"Why do you want so many?"

"They'll come in handy later on. They'll make good cowboys for our cattle ranches."

"Cattle ranches?"

"Well, not cattle, but fish farms, lobster farms, oyster farms, crops of special seaweed that is good to eat."

"Who would eat seaweed?"

"The Japanese eat it all the time. They wrap it around rice, dip it in soy sauce, and love it. It's wholesome and nutritious. And there are a hundred million Japanese—that's a big market right there. And there's no reason why millions of people the world around shouldn't come to like this new food. But that's all in the future. Let's get on with this job of catching big fish."

Shocking Way to Fish

The glass jeep carried the two fishermen near the coral cliff. Here they turned off the motor and waited.

There were thousands of fish poking in the cracks, crevices, caves, and grottoes of the coral precipice, and they were a gorgeous sight in their costumes of red, gold, blue, lavender, and dozens of tints and hues for which there are no names because they are never seen in the world above.

Some of these little beauties were very rare, possibly unknown to science. Aquariums would be glad to get them and would pay well for them. But they were not what Hal wanted just now.

They were all small. Surely a big visitor would be coming along pretty soon. To avoid exhausting their scubas, they breathed the jeep's helium. After a two-hour wait, a large swordfish appeared. Hal took up the electrogun and slipped out of the jeep. He waited for the swordfish to come within range.

But the swordfish was not interested in him or the jeep. It swam idly here and there. It grazed on the plants sprouting from the cliff. It pushed its sword into a hole and brought out an octopus and looked very odd swimming about with eight tentacles wriggling from its beak.

"How can it get it back to its mouth?" Roger wondered.

The swordfish answered by scraping the octopus off against the cliff and caught the squirming thing in its teeth before it could retreat into another hole.

"What kind of a gun is that?" Roger inquired. "Like the dart guns we used in Africa?"

"Not quite," Hal said. "Those darts carried a tranquilizer to put the animal to sleep. This carries electricity."

"How can you fish with electricity? You have the craziest ideas."

"Not so crazy," Hal said. "And it's not really my idea. The Swedes started it. They fish for tuna by electricity. The Norwegians use it for killing whales."

"Oh, I know," said Roger. "You shoot a bomb into a whale, it explodes and blows him to bits."

"No. That was the old way. It destroyed too much of the carcass. Besides, it was very cruel. Sometimes it didn't kill the whale instantly and it swam away before they could fire another charge. Of course a whale is a mammal, like our-selves, and its nerves are as sensitive as ours. So the whale would suffer terribly, for hours, perhaps for weeks. The new way is to shoot a harpoon charged with electricity. It is very sharp and penetrates the hide like a hypodermic without causing pain. And the electric shock kills in-stantly."

Hal had his head up through the hole so that he could carry on this conversation with his brother. Suddenly he dropped down as he saw the swordfish coming straight for the jeep. He raised the electrogun and was about to fire when the swordfish, with a powerful flick of its tail, shot out of range again.

They had already waited two hours; now they waited another hour before Hal could deliver the final blow. The sharp hypodermic did its work and the swordfish lay still.

"But it seems cruel just the same," Roger said.

"Any killing is cruel," said Hal. "You and I prefer to take animals alive. But, remember, just now we are not trying to get animals for a zoo. We are trying to find better ways to get food for people. And you can't get meat without killing. This way of doing it didn't hurt the fish one bit. Don't you think it was a lot better than stabbing the fish with a big hook in its mouth and torturing it for several hours before you can pull it aboard?"

He slipped out with a net which he threw over the swordfish and looped the rope around Bottle's neck. The eager dolphin shot up toward the ship, easily towing the big fish. Hal phoned Captain Ted to stand ready to haul the fish aboard.

But the young naturalist was disappointed with his experiment. He considered it a failure. It had taken three hours to get one fish. Such a slow procedure would never feed the world's hungry millions.

But there was the laser. It was something quite new. He had never used it before. He examined the instrument. It was about the size of a home movie camera.

Roger said, "Is this all there is to it? I don't see any harpoon or gun or anything."

"Yes," Hal said. "This is all there is to it. But it's a pretty wonderful thing. That electrogun isn't much good unless what you're shooting at is not more than thirty feet away. This will reach a hundred thousand miles."

Roger was incredulous. "You're putting me on."

"No, I'm not. Astronauts halfway to the moon could use it to talk to the earth. It sends out a beam of light and a voice can go along on the beam."

"I'll bet anything that could do that will be terribly expensive."

"The first ones were. But an IBM research man, Dr. Peter Sorokin, has invented this cheap model. I bought this for only fifty dollars."

"But what use is it to you? Do you want to talk to the fish?"

"No, but I want to find them. This should help me find them. It works like an echo sounder, only better. It will not only find a big fish, but tell me how far away it is."

"You mean, it talks?"

"Not exactly. It clicks. Listen." He turned on the machine and a ray of light shot forth. At the same time the thing began to click. There was quite a long pause after every click.

"That click goes out along the beam," Hal said, "and if it strikes a large object like a big fish, the echo will come back. And the length of time it takes the echo to come will give us an idea of how far away the fish is. Now, let's go hunting."

He slowly turned the eye of the machine, and the beam began to travel to the right. The clicking continued but for a while there was no answer.

Then suddenly there was an echoing click.

"There's our fish," said Hal excitedly. "Must be a big one, because it's a strong echo. The larger the fish, the better the echo. According to this dial it must be about two miles away."

"But what good is that?" Roger objected. "By the time we get there it will be gone."

"We don't go to it," Hal said. "It will come to us."

Roger stared at him. "What would make it come to us?"

Hal turned a dial and the clicks became very rapid and strong. "A hundred clicks a second," Hal said. "And carried along by the beam, they strike the fish very hard. Fish have a lot of curiosity. When they hear an unusual sound, they come to see what is making it."

"I know that," Roger said. "When we went shark-hunting in the islands we rapped on the side of the boat to attract the shark. It came to see what was making all the noise, and when it got within a few feet of the boat, we would give it the harpoon."

"Yes," Hal said, "and this big fellow is coming fast. The dial shows he has covered a mile in the last few minutes. I'm going to get out with the electrogun and be ready to give him a warm reception when he arrives. Do you think you can operate this thing? Wait until I get this fish—then immediately turn the beam until you get another echo."

"Sure, I can do that," Roger said, proud to have a part in this strange experiment.

Hal dropped into the sea, gun in hand. In an amazingly short time something that looked like a zebra but was twice as large came charging down the light beam. It was more colorful than the zebra. Its stripes were lavender against a silver background, its fins were deep blue, its back was green, and its belly white. Hal recognized the famous striped marlin. A record specimen that had been taken by Zane Grey off Tahiti weighed 1,040 pounds. But nearly all fish of the Great Barrier Reef were larger than those of Tahiti waters and this one was a true monster.

It did not act like the swordfish which had dillydallied around for an hour before it came close enough to be shot. This fellow could not wait to investigate that clicking sound. It came straight to the jeep and did not stop until its bill touched the glass. Hal fired. The electric shock acted instantly and painlessly.

The end of the coil or rope that Hal carried over his shoulder was slipped into the open mouth and out through the gill, then made fast to one of the jet pipes of the jeep.

Roger had already turned the beam and located another echo. This time the distance was much less and it was not two minutes before another big visitor appeared, this time a silver marlin of somewhat smaller size, no heavier than a horse, about five hundred pounds.

Hal easily bagged it, slipped the same rope through mouth and gills, and left it beside its cousin.

He had hardly finished before another marlin hove in sight —evidently this was to be marlin day. This one was the famous Pacific black marlin. The record catch of black marlin weighed 1,226 pounds and was caught in these same waters by a sportsman who struggled most of the day to haul it in.

Any fisherman with rod and line would be very lucky to get one marlin in a day, and it would more likely take a week. Laser had brought in three in ten minutes.

The next was also a black marlin that looked as big as an elephant. It was followed almost at once by a huge grouper with goggle eyes and heavy jaws, an astonished look, and mouth opening and closing that seemed to be saying, "Oh, brother!"

The laser was working well. It picked up only fish that sent back a strong echo, and that meant a big fish every time.

After six more takes, Hal signaled Roger to turn off the beam.

He slipped the rope off the jet and noosed it around the neck of Big Boy in spite of eager whistles from the dolphins who wanted to get in on the game. But this was no job for a dolphin. It took a monster to haul these monsters to the surface.

It was hard work even for the powerful killer whale. He knew where he was supposed to go but found the load almost beyond his strength. Slowly he swam upward. Hal returned to the jeep. He phoned Captain Ted and told him what to expect.

But even with this warning the captain was not prepared for what he saw when Big Boy broke the surface beside the ship with his cargo of monsters. Captain Ted phoned Hal.

"What sort of a joke is this? How do you think I'm going to get these elephants aboard?"

"Use your crane," Hal suggested. "Take up one at a time."

"But where will I put them? The tanks aren't big enough."

"Stow them in the hold," Hal said. "And be ready to take on a lot more."

Hal could hear a deep sigh from the other end of the line. "Fifty years at sea," moaned Captain Ted, "and I've never seen anything like this."

But he was to see a lot more. Within an hour a distress call came down from above. "Let up, will you? The hold is chock-full and every inch of the deck is taken. We're walking around on fish. We're going to sink if we take on any more of these brutes."

Hal laughed. "Okay. Take them to Cairns and deliver them. Use both sails and engine and make a quick trip of it. We'll wait, and have a lot more for you when you get back."

Captain Ted groaned and rang off.

"What do you mean, more?" Roger complained. "Don't you think we've done enough for today?"

Hal smiled. "We've done enough to prove that the laser and electric gun work well together. Any fishing smack can afford to buy a laser. But perhaps it won't be equipped with the electric shock apparatus. I want to see if the laser alone will do the trick."

Roger looked puzzled. "The laser pulls them in all right. But it doesn't kill them."

"I think perhaps it will if we turn up the power," Hal said. "In medicine, laser is used to cure some diseases. For instance, there's a very bad tumor, something like cancer. It's called melanoma. At the Pasadena Tumor Institute they use laser to kill melanoma. It takes only a very weak beam and only a thousandth of a second."

"What does curing that thingamajig have to do with killing fish?"

"The reason for using a weak beam is that a strong one would kill both the tumor and the patient. We've been using a very weak beam to bring in these fish. But suppose when the fish arrives we suddenly turn on the strong beam. Of course these big chaps are much more powerful than a human and they may be able to stand the shock. I don't know—that's what we'll find out."

They soon found out. The low-power beam brought in the fish. At the last moment when the inquisitive fish nosed the jeep, the laser was switched to high power, and the fish, without knowing what had struck it, passed out.

Long before Captain Ted telephoned that he had come back from the twenty-mile trip to Cairns, there was another big load waiting to go aboard.

This time neither the dolphins nor the killer whale were to have the fun of towing the catch to the surface.

"Break out the balloons," Hal said. "I think we'll need three."

"What are the balloons for?"

"To do the same job that the dolphins and Big Boy are doing."

"But if they can do it, why use balloons?"

"We have to think of all the possibilities," Hal said. "Let's suppose you are the captain of a fishing smack. You may be able to train dolphins to help you, or you may not. Or perhaps there are no dolphins in the seas where you are working. Your divers round up the fish by laser, but how are you going to get them to the ship?"

"I see," said Roger. "But you can't use balloons for that. They work only in the air."

"What makes you think so?"

"Because I've seen them in the air, but never underwater."

"But why don't they work underwater? They work in the air because we fill them with gas that is lighter than air. They should work underwater if we fill them with gas that is lighter than water."

"What gas?"

"Any gas. Air itself is a gas, and it's a lot lighter than water."

He took up the bottle of compressed air that Captain Ted had sent down. "This is air under great pressure and it will expand enough to fill three balloons. I'll go out, and you can hand me the balloons one at a time."

Hal went under and Roger passed him the first balloon. Hal roped together about a dozen of the big fish and made fast the rope to the balloon. Then he latched the air bottle to the balloon nozzle and turned on the valve.

The balloon filled at once and lifted so powerfully that Hal could no longer hold it. Up it went, towing the heavy load.

Hal returned to the jeep. "Phone the captain," he said. "And pass me another balloon."

Another haul of fish went up with the second balloon, and the final lot with the third. Altogether, the boys had taken several hundred great groupers, barracudas, wahoos, cobias, giant mullets, dorados, and albacores—all good food fish.

The distressed voice of Captain Ted came over the radiophone. "You're driving us wild. What do we do with all these?"

"Take them in to the packing plant," Hal said. "They'll know what to do with them."

What the city of Cairns could not use could be shipped by train to the towns of the Australian coast all the way from Cape York at the northern tip to Melbourne in the south. Or they could be canned to go to India or any other part of the hungry world.

The important thing was not this great haul of fish, but the fact that ways had been opened up for the fishing industry everywhere to increase its output perhaps a hundredfold. But only if fishing captains everywhere knew of the success of these experiments. Hal knew that Dr. Dick would eagerly take care of that by his reports to scientific journals and journals of the fishing industry.

That was up to Dr. Dick. The boys were already impatient to get on to something else.

"What'll we do now?" demanded Roger.

"Well," said Hal, looking out at several writhing, twisting, evil-looking things close to the jeep, "if you don't mind doing something a bit more dangerous, let's go play with snakes."

Sea Snakes

Roger was not bubbling with enthusiasm over the idea of playing with snakes.

"They don't look like good playmates," he said. "But I suppose they can't really do any harm."

"I don't know why you suppose that," said Hal. "Of course there are many kinds of sea snakes and some of them just swim away. But the ones along the Great Barrier Reef are not so meek and mild. They are big—those outside seem to be about ten feet long. And they would as soon bite you as not. They are supposed to have the same ancestor as the cobra and krait. The venom of one species is fifty times as strong as the king cobra's."

"Then why do you want to fool with them?"

"Because one of the most important things we have to do is to collect poisonous animals for laboratories."

"What can they do with them?"

"Extract the poison. You know how they milk a snake to get the venom. Then they use the venom to make antivenin to cure snakebite. But they also use all sorts of poisons from snakes, fish, jellyfish, sea wasps, and many other sea creatures to make medicines good for all sorts of diseases. So far as I know, no such collection of venomous animals has been made in the waters of the Great Barrier Reef."

Roger understood. "I get you," he said. "Let's go. How do we kill them?"

"We don't kill them. We take them alive. If we kill them, the poison would spoil before we could get them to the labs."

Roger looked closely at the sea snakes. "You say their granddaddies were cobras. They don't look much like cobras to me. See how broad and flat their tails are. Besides, how could they be descended from cobras? The cobra is a land snake."

"So were these—once. They used to live on land. Then, for some reason they took a fancy to go to sea."

"How do you know that?"

"We know it because they have lungs, not gills. They breathe air. They can stay down for a long time, even for hours, but then they must come up to breathe."

"But," objected Roger, "no land snakes have broad tails like those. How do you explain that?"

"Well," Hal said, "think of the dolphins. They once walked around on land. But when they came to the sea their feet gradually changed into fins and their tails became wide and flat so they could push themselves through the water. The tails of those snakes are now powerful paddles that can shoot them through the water at tremendous speed."

Now there were more snakes than ever. Some were darting at the jeep as if trying to get at the luscious morsels inside. Their fangs thudded against the glass.

"Come to think of it," Hal said, "I believe you had better stay inside."

Roger screwed up his courage enough to say, "Not on your life. If you can take it, so can I." He was done with being considered the baby of the family. He was big for his age and almost as strong as his brother.

"All right," Hal said reluctantly, "but you know how to take a snake?"

"Sure. You grab it behind the head."

"And hang on," Hal added. "They're strong. They'll twist away from you and bite if they can."

"Enough instructions," Roger said. "Let's get going."

They slid out through the hatch. The snakes scattered. Probably they had never known sea monsters like these and were a little afraid of them. But they were very curious. Or hungry. They would attack other sea animals of all sizes, so why not these?

They swam about with their jaws open. Their hollow, poison-filled fangs did not lie down like the fangs of some snakes, but stood erect like those of the cobra. Their forked tongues darted in and out.

They were really a gorgeous sight, evidently of several different varieties. Some were yellow-bellied, some a dazzling blue, some brown with yellow bands or yellow with black bands. Both boys had seen enough snakes in their father's zoo to appreciate their beauty, and they had taken snakes alive in Africa, but never before beneath the sea. These creatures were so much at home underwater and glided about with such ease that the boys who had not spent millions of years beneath the waves felt clumsy and out of place. These were their air-breathing cousins—but cousins far removed.

They swarmed around the boys, staring at them with big beady eyes. Why was their stare so menacing? Roger decided it was because they never blinked their eyelids. Then he saw that there was good reason why they never blinked—they had no eyelids. And they had no ear openings. They heard (or rather felt) with their tongues. Those darting tongues looked dangerous. But Roger knew that even the tongue of a poisonous snake is quite harmless. The tongue is used to detect sounds, just as the nerves in the lateral line down the side of a fish are sensitive to any sound.

One big snake, after due inspection of these strange creatures, resolved to try its luck. It shot in and closed its fangs on the seat of Hal's bathing suit. It squirted some of its poison into the cloth, then waited for this big animal to die. Its teeth had certainly penetrated what it supposed to be the skin of this beast, and by all the rules of snakedom the poison should spread through the body, causing terrible convulsions, and death.

It was doubtless quite surprised when things didn't work out as it had planned. Instead, it suddenly felt a choking grip around its throat just back of the head.

Hal jerked it loose from the cloth and stuffed it, wriggling violently, into a plastic sack he had brought with him.

Three more snakes charged in and joined the others in the sack. Roger had not yet had a visitor.

But now he found himself unable to move his right leg. Perhaps he had been bitten and had not felt it. Hal had told him that the fang of a sea snake is so sharp that the bite is not felt. Roger went cold with fear. He tried again to move his leg. Surely he had been bitten and the leg was numb. The numbness would spread and soon he would not be able to move a muscle. Then the terrible pains would start.

He could still swim with his left leg, but the right one was no good. Soon the left also would go back on him. He was sorry now that he had been so cocky. He should have stayed in the jeep as his brother advised.

He put his hand down and gripped his right leg. Much to his surprise, he felt the pressure of his fingers. The leg was not numb after all. Then what was the trouble? Had he caught his foot in a tangle of seaweed?

It is not easy to see in all directions through a face mask, but he managed to look down and saw the answer to the mystery of the wooden leg. A snake nine feet long had buried its fangs in the rubber of his flipper.

Roger tried to kick it off, but the weight of the big snake was enough to hold the leg rigid. Roger swatted the unwelcome visitor with his other fin. With the fin he tried to scrape it off, but it hung on like grim death.

Then he reached down, took it by the neck, and pulled. It came loose, taking a piece of the fin with it.

It began whipping about, and Roger could hardly hold it. Hal saw what had happened and came with the sack. Before he could get to his brother, the snake had wound itself tightly around Roger's arm. Luckily it was not a constrictor like a boa or python and was not in the habit of squeezing its victims to death. It trusted its poison fangs to do this deadly work.

Roger tried to tear it off with his other hand. Hal had joined him now and both boys exerted all their strength to pull away the black and yellow coils. Finally it came loose and Roger stuffed it into the bag. But as he let go of the neck the snake twisted its head and one fang brushed against his hand.

It was just a scrape and Roger thought nothing of it. He was greatly relieved to get this pest safe in the sack.

Hal put his hand on Roger's arm and drew him back to the jeep. They climbed in.

"Let me see that," Hal said.

"It's nothing," said Roger.

"Let me see it anyway."

"It's only a scratch. Look."

A drop of blood was welling from the scratch.

Hal brushed away the blood. He put his mouth to the slight abrasion, sucked hard, then spat. He sucked again and again until he was blue in the face.

"A lot of monkey business about nothing," Roger said.

"I'm not so sure of that," said Hal. "You didn't get much. It won't be enough to finish you off. But it may be enough to make you mighty uncomfortable. Wish we had some antiserum. But it hasn't been invented yet."

"I thought you had some."

"For land-snake bite—not sea snake. If you had just waited until we could get these snakes to a lab and get some antiserum back . . . But you were in too much of a hurry."

In spite of his joking manner, Hal was worried. He had tied a tourniquet of rope around the wrist above the scratch. He must release it every thirty minutes. He continued the mouth-to-hand treatment.

"I don't feel a thing," Roger said, "except a little stiffness."

Hal looked at him anxiously. "That's the first sign of trouble," he said.

"But it isn't my hand that is stiff. It's my legs."

"That's the way it starts," Hal said. "Funny, how a bit of poison in your hand can make your legs stiff. Then the stiffness slowly goes up through your body."

"Perhaps I'd better exercise my legs to keep them limber."

"No. Lie still. I'd better get you back to the house and into bed."

"Bed nothing. You're making a big thing out of nothing."

But Hal was already at the controls. He put on full power and the jeep sped to town. Arriving home, he helped Roger out of his clothes and into bed.

By this time the stiffness had risen to the neck. It climbed farther to the jaws. It might cause lockjaw. Roger could speak only with difficulty and complained that he could hardly swallow. But he wanted to swallow because there was a burning or dryness in his throat and he was uncommonly thirsty.

Hal took his pulse. It was not fast, but it was weak and irregular.

The poison had reached the eyes. The pupils were dilated and the eyelids drooped.

Then the pains began. The muscles of Roger's arms and legs jumped and twitched. It seemed to Roger that every nerve in his body was hopping. Spasms of pain ran through him from head to toe. Hal found that the patient's skin was cold and clammy. He covered him with another blanket.

The next hour was pure torture. Convulsions racked the poisoned body. Roger had never known such suffering. He wanted to scream. But men did not scream. Trying to control himself, he bit his lip until it bled. He could hardly breathe. He felt as if an elephant were sitting on his chest.

The convulsions suddenly ended when he became unconscious. Hal anxiously put his fingers on the boy's pulse. He could feel nothing.

After a few moments there was a slight throb, then a very feeble beat. It was come and go. It would stop for as much as ten seconds and begin again.

Finally the boy passed from unconsciousness into normal sleep. The heartbeat became stronger. This lad was a tough customer—he wouldn't die easily. Hal sat by his bed all night.

He was ready to give up his search for poisons to be turned into medicines. The idea had seemed good, but now he hated it. It was a thing that ought to be done, but why not let others do it?

Roger slept late the next morning. When he opened his eyes, the pupils were back to normal and there was no droop in the eyelids. He lay quietly without any sign of pain.

"You poor boob," he said. "How long have you been sitting there?"

"Awhile," said Hal. "How do you feel?"

"Just fine. Rarin' to go."

He threw off the covers, got up, and began to dress.

"Hadn't you better stay quiet?"

"I don't know why," Roger said. " 'Fraid I've been wasting a lot of time, lying there half the day when there's so much to do."

"There's nothing to do," Hal said.

"But your poisons?" said Roger.

Hal said, "We're quitting all that. We'll find something else to do."

Roger scolded, "Listen, big brother, you don't need to baby me. Don't tell me you're quitting. You're no quitter, and neither am I. I tell you I'm all right. I bet you haven't had breakfast yet, and I'm hungry too. Let's have a snack, then get back to our nice little poisons."

The Floating Death

So they went out again, looking for trouble.

There was no lack of that under the sea. Plenty of beauty, plenty of trouble. Thousands of harmless and lovely angels such as the angelfish and moorish idols. Hundreds of ugly creatures that looked and acted like the devil.

Some were both beautiful and devilish.

The first the boys saw was one of the handsomest creatures of the sea. It had as many gorgeous plumes as an Indian chief's headdress.

"It looks like a bird of paradise," Roger said.

"Yes," said his brother. "Or a peacock. But those fine feathers conceal stingers full of poison. Especially at the back end of the fish."

"What good do they do back there? I should think he'd have them up at the business end."

"The back end *is* the business end. And it's really a very clever arrangement. Any fish would expect the danger to be up front. This rascal takes them by surprise. When he sees some creature he wants to eat, he passes and goes ahead of it. The fish he is after thinks it is safe and pays no more attention. Then suddenly the lion-fish shoots backward and stabs it with his rear spines. The poison promptly kills the fish, and the lion-fish can feast upon it at leisure."

"Why do they call it the lion-fish?"

"Because some people think its plumes look like the mane of a lion. I'll go get it."

"Let me," Roger said.

Before his brother could object, he grabbed his sack and slid out of the jeep.

The lion-fish took an interest in him at once. It came close and studied him with big eyes. Then it pretended to have other business, and passed him. It stopped and drifted. Then it came back like a bolt of lightning going the wrong way.

Roger slid out of its path at the last instant and held the sack with its mouth wide open. The lion-fish shot into it tail first and Roger flipped the bag shut. He tied it to one of the legs of the jeep and got back inside. The whole operation had not taken two minutes.

Hal congratulated him. "Pretty neat," he said. "There's a sea wasp. This time it's my turn."

"But that's only a jellyfish. Does it have any poison?"

"I'll say it has. The sea wasp has killed a lot of people along the Australian coast. Some scientists say it's the most venomous marine animal known. A boy twelve years old up near Darwin was swimming when one of these things showed up just ahead of him. He thought it was harmless and brushed it away. He died in seven minutes. Another swimmer was finished in three minutes. He was pulled out with the sea wasp still clinging to his dead body. When they pulled it off, the skin came with it. Always look out for jellyfish. Most of them won't do you a bit of harm except perhaps give you an itchy skin, but there are a few that are downright murder.

And when you can't tell which are the bad ones, it's best to avoid them all."

The sea wasp wasn't going anywhere. It didn't need to. All it had to do was to wait until something brushed through its tentacles.

It happened very soon. A fish as large as the sea wasp itself wandered into the stingers and lay dead. Then the sea wasp performed a miracle. It protruded its stomach, wrapped the fish in its folds, and drew it inside. It expanded to accommodate this meal and was twice as big as before. As it digested the fish it would shrink to its former size.

When Hal came out, it made no effort to move away. The mushy body was scooped up without difficulty and another bag was tied to the jeep.

"Be nice if everything were as easy as that," Hal said when he returned.

Roger spied a pretty shell on a ledge of the reef. He instantly dropped out and was astonished when he was grabbed by the hair and pulled back into the jeep.

"What did you do that for?" he demanded.

"Before you grab that shell, I want to tell you something about it. That's a cone shell."

"You don't need to tell me about cone shells. I've picked up lots of them."

"But not that kind. There are more than four hundred species of cone shells, but only six of them are very poisonous. This is one of them."

"But it's so small, it can't really be bad."

"It is bad—one of the worst. It's called a marbled cone because it looks like patterned marble. Go ahead and get it but take it by the large end. The small end is open and just inside there is a little black animal with a stinger like a harpoon that it is ready to jab into anything that comes along."

"It must be a very tiny stinger," said Roger. "How could that hurt you?"

"It's connected with a sac of deadly poison. One little squirt of that, and you would be dead."

"Aren't you exaggerating?"

"Not a bit. An Australian boy walking on top of the reef when it is bare at low tide picked up one of these and held it in his closed hand. The thing stung him on his finger. The poison acted so fast that he was dead in three minutes. Now, go ahead, but take it by the large end."

Roger left the jeep and swam close to the ledge. The shell looked so harmless. It was only about an inch and a half long. The large end was closed, the small end was the front door. It was a tiny opening, no bigger than the head of a pin. Roger could not see inside the hole.

He took out his knife and tapped on the shell. Instantly what looked like a black needle came out of the hole. Finding nothing to murder, it drew back into the shell.

Roger picked up the shell by the large end and held it gingerly as he swam back to the jeep.

"Wish I had a toothpick," Hal said.

"What do you want with a toothpick?"

"To plug up that hole. Of course out of water the thing will die—but that will take some hours. In the meantime it's a dangerous thing to have lying around. You might put your hand or foot on it and then good night. When we get home, we'll plug the hole shut with a toothpick or chewing gum or whatever else we have handy. A lab will be glad to get this. Its poison is more powerful, drop for drop, than the poison of a big land snake. And it can be converted into a number of different medicines."

"I still can't understand," Roger said, "how something that can kill you can be made into something that can cure you."

Hal agreed. "We don't pretend to understand it. Even the

lab men don't. But it works. Just as the bad-smelling stuff a civet cat shoots out can be made into perfume, or garbage can be made into soap. Perhaps there's nothing in the world that is altogether bad."

The search for bad-good fish continued. It was not hard to find them. Possibly nowhere else in the world was there so great a gathering of sea creatures as along the face of the Great Barrier Reef.

The sea scorpion was added to the collection.

"Boy, is it ugly," said Roger. "Like something out of a nightmare."

"Ugly and edible," said Hal. "The French consider it very good to eat. They make one of their famous soups out of it."

"Where is the stinger?" Roger asked, examining the specimen they had captured.

"In a very strange place. It's underneath. Instead of killing its victims by shooting forward or backward, it surprises them by dropping down on them."

"The sea is full of surprises," said Roger.

"I'll say it is," agreed Hal.

The stonefish, so ugly that it is called the "horrida," was added to the collection. It is also called "the waiting one" because it doesn't move from morning to night. It simply lies on the ground waiting for someone to make a mistake. It is about the color of the sea bottom and is usually half concealed by mud or sand. A man wading or swimming is very likely to step on it, and the poisonous spines that stand up from its warty back stab his foot. Fish grazing along the bottom for food suddenly become food for the stonefish when they are stabbed by the spines which then bend to push them over into the great mouth.

The boys did not make the mistake of stepping on it. That was the mistake of a crab which crawled over the waiting one only to be caught on the spines and promptly eaten.

Although it did not move, catching it was a delicate matter. You could not grab it by the spiny back. When Hal tried to pick it up by the tail, it clung to the rock beneath.

Roger brought the jeep into position so that its iron claw could close on the stonefish. Then he backed the jeep and pulled the thing loose. Hal held a sack open below the victim, Roger opened the iron jaws, and the horrida was bagged.

Both boys breathed a sigh of relief. "I'm glad that's over," Hal said. "Just one little jab from those spines and if you didn't die you might go insane and spend the rest of your life wandering around as crazy as a loon. It's the chief cause of insanity among the islanders of the South Seas."

The jeep was now within two feet of the reef, and through its glass wall they could see the reef builders at work. Some people suppose that you have to have a microscope to see these tiny coral animals, called polyps. This is not always true. The polyps are different sizes. Some are no larger than pinheads. Some are half an inch wide and can be plainly seen with their flowerlike tentacles extended, each polyp sitting in a cup of limestone secreted from its own body.

The word "polyp" sounds as if the thing might be a bit of pulp or plant growth, not the well-constructed and efficient animal that it is. It gathers food, builds a house for itself, poisons unwelcome visitors, and erects a monument far greater than the Washington Monument or the Taj Mahal.

All about the boys was an underwater paradise. They looked down on a dream forest. Imagine a twenty-foot tree bearing only one leaf twenty feet broad. It and a hundred like it had been built by the small coral animal. Under the shadow of the great leaf hundreds of brilliant little fish flitted like butterflies.

And there was something that looked like the banyan, a tree with a hundred trunks like the columns in a cathedral. It was densely covered with coral leaves, and under them a scuba diver might easily get lost exploring the submarine labyrinth.

This part of the ocean floor did not look like a floor, but like the top of a fantastic woodland seen from an airplane—a jungle of trees of all sizes. What a thrill to look down between the weird branches into these blue and purple canyons, where tiny flecks of color shot in and out among the twigs while bigger and more solemn fish swam slowly near the bottom.

The colors looked delicate and the stone leaves fragile, and it was an odd sensation when the jeep bumped against one and found it as hard as rock.

It was not all so lovely. On one of the stone branches lay a horrible-looking creature which Hal identified as a sea centipede. It looked as unpleasant as the land centipede, so unpleasant that even an animal lover could not like it. It had perhaps a hundred legs—the boys didn't attempt to count them. The most frightening thing about it was its size. The centipede one sees on land may be only two or three inches long. This watery cousin was a good two feet. Another one crawled along nearby.

"I think we want both of those," Hal said. "One to send to a lab and the other to eat."

Roger's face crinkled in disgust. "Who could ever eat that thing?"

"You and I could," said Hal. "And will. You'll like it. It's even better than lobster. It is called a varo, and the Polynesians like it so much that they frequently name a son Varo. Then every time they look at him they think of the delicious sea centipede."

"What good is one to a lab?"

"Every one of those feet is full of poison. The centipede will tackle even a large fish, dig its claws into it, paralyze it with poison, and then eat it."

Here again the iron claw was useful. It clutched one of the

centipedes, tore it loose from its hundred-foot grip on the coral branch, and dropped it into the bag that was this time held by Roger. In the same way, the other joined its mate in the bag.

"We'll have to be careful when we cook it," Hal said. "Those claws cut like scissors and the poison makes wounds that will fester and swell for weeks."

"How nice," Roger said. "I think I'll leave the cooking to you—and the eating, too."

"How generous you are," said Hal.

Roger dismissed it with a wave of his hand. "Don't mention it. Just call it brotherly love."

The climax of the poison hunt was "The Floating Death," as it is called by some Australians. Elsewhere it is known as the Portuguese man-of-war.

The boys noticed first that the water had turned light blue. Then they saw that the color came from dozens of tentacles trailing down from the surface. They were attached to what looked like a bright blue boat. The tentacles were at least thirty feet long.

"There's the best prize of the day," said Hal, "if we can just get it. Those tentacles carry a lot of poison and, believe it or not, electric batteries. The thing up there that looks like a boat is really a big blue bag filled with gas."

"It seems to be moving away," Roger said.

"Put on low power and follow it. It has a sail on top of the bag and the wind moves it slowly along."

"Those tentacles can't be so bad," said Roger. "I see some little blue-black fish swimming in among them."

Hal said, "Those little fish are the man-of-war's buddies. It leaves them alone. Other fish see them there and are fooled into thinking the tentacles are harmless. They plunge in after the little fellows, get tangled up in the tentacles, and get both electric shock and poison. Then they are gathered up to the hungry mouth of the man-of-war."

Roger was puzzled. "I don't see how you're going to take it. If it were near the ship, the captain might snare it and pull it aboard. But the wind has carried it a good distance and we've gone with it. Besides, it's such a sprawly thing, and all those long tentacles! I think we can find something that will be easier to get."

"We're going to get this," Hal said. "But it's a job for two men—one to hold a coil of rope and the other to pass the end of the rope around the bunch of tentacles. Then Bottle can tow it to the ship."

"I'll bet it won't be as simple as it sounds," said Roger. But he took up a coil of rope, and both adventurers left the jeep and swam close to the dangerous dangle of blue tentacles. Roger held the coil while Hal looped the end around the stringy mass and tied it.

So far, so good. The faithful Bottle, as usual, was close at hand. Hal gave the free end of the rope to Bottle who at once understood what he was supposed to do.

He swam off toward the ship. But even a dolphin can make mistakes. In his eagerness to carry out his errand he drew the twitching ends of the tentacles straight over Hal's body.

The tentacles at once wrapped themselves around the naturalist's back and chest. Hal felt a series of quick electric jolts. He knew that thousands of tiny darts were pouring poison into him. He struggled to get away but was firmly held.

Roger ventured close and at the risk of getting stung himself seized Hal's foot and tried to pull him loose. It didn't work.

What to do now? As fast as he could he swam back to the jeep, powered it up, and brought it near enough so that the iron claw could grip Hal's arm. Then he backed away.

With the dolphin pulling in one direction and the iron claw

in the opposite direction, Hal felt as if he were about to be pulled apart. But the powerful engine succeeded in pulling him free of the strings of death. In doing so, the ends of the tentacles were broken and stuck to the boy's body with their darts penetrating the skin and administering more poison.

At first there had been terrifying pains. Now the pains were dying down. This was a bad sign. Hal knew it meant that he was being paralyzed. The paralysis was numbing his nerves so that he could no longer feel.

He could hardly make it back to the jeep. Roger hauled him in. Hal muttered, "Phone the captain to watch for Bottle."

Roger did so. "Now," Hal said, "get these things off me."

Roger slipped on a pair of rubber gloves and tried to strip off the blue strings of poison. They stuck so tightly to the flesh that he could not get them loose. "Can't do it," he said.

"You've got to. If they don't come off, I'm dead. Dig them off with your knife."

This was not a job to Roger's liking, but he went to work. With the sharp end of his knife he cut into the flesh below a tentacle and managed to pry it loose, pulling out of the skin the hundreds of little barbed hooks. Of course the flesh came with them, and as each tentacle was dug away it left a track of blood.

Hal was hopelessly dizzy and nauseated. His mind began fogging over. His eyes were glazed and his teeth clenched. His chest tightened up until it was as hard as a board. That meant his lungs were being paralyzed. His breath came in gasps.

"What else can I do?" Roger said in despair.

"Nothing. Get me back to the house."

Returning home, Roger somehow got him out of the jeep and up into the house, where he lay on the floor while Roger sponged away the blood trails and applied some antiseptic.

He wrapped a towel around his brother and helped him struggle into bed.

The patient was still conscious, but it was so hard to breathe that he feared he would suffocate.

"Be ready," he managed to mumble, "to give me artificial respiration."

Dr. Roger Hunt was at his wits' end. His medical knowledge was too slight and he was painfully aware of his own ignorance. His brother was feverish, so he laid a wet rag over the hot forehead.

What would he do if his brother died? He knew that death was possible. He remembered the news report of the Australian boy who had been attacked, managed to pull himself loose, swam fifty yards to shore, then collapsed and died. A fourteen-year-old girl at Kissing Point Baths, Australia, made it to the hospital but died a day later. Just the electric shock alone was serious, without counting the poison. It was like being wrapped in high-powered electric lines.

The phone rang. It was the captain. He said, "Bottle is alongside with the man-of-war. What will I do with it?"

"Hoist it aboard with the derrick," Roger said. "Give it a tank all to itself."

"But its tentacles hang down thirty feet," objected the captain. "And our tanks are only ten feet deep."

"Can't help that," Roger said. "It will just have to spread its tentacles out over the floor of the tank."

"But that's not natural for a man-of-war. It will be mighty uncomfortable."

"I don't give a hoot if it's uncomfortable," exclaimed Roger. "It nearly killed my brother." And he told the captain what had happened.

"That's bad," said Captain Ted. "Did you put on the shaving cream?"

"Shaving cream!" exploded Roger. "I don't think that's funny."

"I didn't intend it to be. Shaving cream is the old remedy for man-of-war stings."

"Well, I'll do it," said Roger doubtfully. "But do you think I d better get him to the hospital?"

"No. He shouldn't be moved. You've done everything they could do—except the shaving cream. In fact, I think you're a pretty good doctor. But get the cream on right away. Then keep him quiet. He'll come out of it."

Roger got the tube of shaving cream and rubbed in a streak of it along every cut.

He could only hope that the captain knew what he was talking about. He should know, for he had spent his life along this coast where the man-of-war was a well-known pest.

Kaggs came in. "What's the matter with your brother?"

"Tangled with a man-of-war," Roger said.

"Oh, now, isn't that just too bad?" But somehow Kaggs didn't look too sorry. In fact, there was something that seemed like a gleam of satisfaction in his eyes. "Suppose I take over. What he needs is some exercise."

Hal's eyes were closed. He was either unconscious or asleep. The captain had said to keep him still.

Kaggs started toward the bed. "Leave him alone," Roger said.

Kaggs looked astonished. "Now, my boy, don't tell me what to do. Remember, I'm a bit older than you, and perhaps a little wiser. We should wake him up and give him a workout."

"Don't touch him," said Roger angrily. "If you do I'll knock your head off."

Kaggs stared. "Well, of all the impudence!" Then he adopted his most oily manner. "I'll have to excuse you for your impertinence. I understand how disturbed you must be." He started again toward the bed.

Suddenly Hal's eyes opened and he sat up. Except for a little stiffness, his paralysis was gone. He almost sang, he was so happy to be alive. He ached all over his chest and back as if he had a first-degree burn. But he could breathe and he could move. Seeing Kaggs, he said, "Thanks for all you did. Whatever it was, it was the right thing. I feel fine."

Kaggs smiled. "I'm glad I got here just in time. I'm sure you'll be all right now." He went to his room.

"Well, of all the nerve!" said Roger. But he was so grateful for his brother's recovery that he didn't bother to tell him Kaggs had done nothing.

How to Make an Enemy

Hal was reporting to Dr. Dick.

"Some of my experiments worked out," he said. "Some didn't. We tried underwater fishing. Our bottle-nose dolphin —we called him Bottle—learned very quickly to run errands for us to our ship, *Flying Cloud*. My brother made friends with a killer whale and he hauls up loads that would be too heavy for the dolphin. Other dolphins have joined in, so now we have a team of twenty of them, and I believe they can be trained to serve as cowboys to guard the animal farms, fish farms, oyster beds, lobster fields, and this and that that we're planning."

"If you can do that," Dr. Dick said, "it will be a long step ahead. Single dolphins have been used before this, but I don't recall any experiment with a team of dolphins."

"Well," Hal said, "we may fail—just as we failed with the electric shock."

"Electric shock? What was that?"

"Not an original idea," Hal replied. "As you know, for

some years whalers have been using the electric harpoon to kill whales painlessly. Of course they do that from a surface ship. Whales come to the surface to breathe, but big fish don't usually come up; so they were safe from the electric harpoon. But if you could go down where they are, the electric harpoon could be used. We tried it, and it failed. I'm sorry we wasted so much time on an experiment that we should have known wouldn't work."

"Why didn't it work?"

"It worked if a big fish came around. But we might wait for half an hour or an hour before a big fellow happened to come by. That was no better than a fishing boat could do with a hook and line or a net. So we tried laser."

Dr. Dick looked worried. "But a laser machine costs five or ten thousands dollars. I'm not sure that we could afford such an expense."

"A new one has been invented," Hal said. "It cost only fifty dollars. And John Hunt and Sons paid for it, because we can use it in our own work."

"But how can you use laser for fishing?"

"The laser beam carries a clicking sound along with it, and when it strikes a big object such as a large fish, the fish, out of curiosity, comes to see what is making the noise. When the fish came close, we finished him off with the electric shock. We got more fish that way in half an hour than fishermen up on top would be apt to get in a day or perhaps even a week."

"Great," smiled Dr. Dick. "Any fishing smack could afford to buy a laser at that price. But suppose it didn't have the electric harpoon apparatus and no trained dolphin or killer whale to bring up the fish?"

Hal admired Dr. Dick's quick mind. "You're quite right. So we tried laser alone—no electric business and no finny errand boys. We brought in the fish by low-power laser, and when they came close, we finished them off by turning on high power. Then we sent them up by balloon instead of by dolphin or whale."

Dr. Dick grinned. "Very ingenious!" he said. "What other magic have you been practicing?"

"Nothing really magical," Hal said modestly. "We've been picking up some poisons to send to laboratories that use them in making medicines."

"You mean poisonous fish?"

"Yes—like the sea snake, lion-fish, scorpion fish, cone shell, sea wasp, stonefish, sea centipede, and man-of-war."

"But isn't that pretty dangerous work?"

"Not too bad," Hal said, thinking it unnecessary to relate how both he and Roger had nearly lost their lives.

A head bobbed up through a hole in the other room. It was followed by the body of a young man who stood dripping while he gazed around until his eyes rested upon the two men in the study.

He removed the scuba mouthpiece from his mouth and said, "Is Dr. Dick here?"

"I'm Dr. Dick," said the director.

"May I speak to you for a few moments?"

"Come right in."

Hal disliked the face. The eyes were shifty and too close together, the chin was weak and flabby, the mouth had a mean twist at the corners.

"My name is Oscar Roach," he said. "I came to see about getting a job."

"In what capacity?"

"Naturalist," said Roach.

Dr. Dick rose and shook hands. "Meet our present naturalist, Hal Hunt," he said.

Hal shook hands. "Glad to know you," he said.

Roach did not reply. Instead, he seemed highly displeased.

"If you'll excuse me, gentlemen," Hal said, "I must be running along."

After he had gone, Roach said, "So—you already have a naturalist. Guess I'm here on a wild-goose chase."

"Sorry," said Dr. Dick, "but the job is filled. Pretty well filled." And he went on to tell Roach of some of Hal's experiments.

"Then I suppose you have no opening for me?"

"Not as naturalist. But I might find some other assignment for you. Do you have any references?"

Roach looked flustered by the question. His face went red. "I don't have any with me," he admitted.

"But you have had other jobs?"

"Lots of them."

That didn't sound too good to Dr. Dick. If a man has had lots of jobs, it means that he wasn't able to hold one very long.

"I can fit you in," he said. "But it would be a minor job."

"Doing what?"

"They need a dishwasher over at the hotel."

Roach looked angry but he said nothing. "Of course," Dr. Dick went on, "it would be just temporary. If Hunt should drop out for any reason, you would be considered next in line to take his place."

If Hunt should drop out. If Hunt should drop out. Dr. Dick should have been able to see it going round and round in Roach's mind.

"I'll take the dishwashing job," he said.

Roger's Little Joke

They had never seen a shark as big as this one.

First it passed over the jeep like a black cloud. Then circled and came down to study this strange glass thing more closely. It was a good fifty feet long. Its open mouth was six feet wide.

"That's a whale shark," said Hal excitedly. "Greatest of all the sharks. You can tell it by the white spots on its hide. And by the croaks—hear it?"

The croaking sounds of the monster were quite audible. "It's the only talking shark," Hal said.

"There don't seem to be any teeth in that mouth," said Roger.

"No, it doesn't bite or chew its food. It just inhales it. It goes along with its mouth open and anything in the way goes down the hatch. Mainly it lives on plankton—those tiny bits of animal life in the sea. It's not supposed to be vicious like most sharks. It even allows a man to ride on its back. Or so they say—I wouldn't like to chance it."

"I would," said the venturesome Roger, and before Hal

could stop him he slipped out of the jeep. The monster lay still, evidently much interested in this big glass bubble. Roger swam up beside it.

What a whale of a shark! No wonder they called it the whale shark. Paste three elephants together and they would not be as big as this brute.

Roger touched its rough flank, but it did not seem to notice him. He mustered up the courage to tickle it under the chin. It seemed to like it.

He swam up to the top of the back, like the roof of a house. He sat down. You couldn't straddle this thing—you had to sit Turkish fashion. It was like sitting on the deck of a ship.

The ship began to move—very slowly. It circled the jeep, looking at it from every angle. It seemed to be undecided whether to swallow it or not. But it apparently gave up the idea. Glass bubbles were not its favorite dish. Again it came to a halt and just lay, looking.

A stream of small sea bits kept flowing into the creature's mouth. Evidently there was quite a lot of suction there—like the suction of a vacuum cleaner.

Roger swam around to examine this cavernous mouth. It was quite as big as a telephone booth. Since there were no teeth, Roger felt safe. And since the monster appeared to have a habit of keeping its mouth open, why shouldn't he explore this cave more completely?

He felt the suction and allowed it to carry him in. This was a new sensation—sitting on the inside of a fish. That story about Jonah inside the great fish, possibly it was true after all. Though how Jonah stayed alive without breathing was a mystery. Roger, inhaling from his aqualung, had no such difficulty. He was quite comfortable; and he could leave the great open mouth whenever he chose. It was like being in a submarine with an open hatch.

He could see Hal madly gesturing him to come out. But why should he come out just yet? He was enjoying this strange experience.

He was considerably surprised when the mouth began to close. The monster had evidently come to the conclusion that it had a big-enough mouthful. Roger tried to get out before the jaws came shut, but it was impossible.

With the mouth closed, the cave was as dark as a pocket. Still Roger was not frightened. Hal had said that the whale shark was not mean like other sharks.

But someone was frightened, and that was Hal. He swam to the shark's head and began to beat on its mouth with the handle of his knife. He might as well have beaten a stone wall. To the shark, his blows were like love pats. It did not even flick its tail which stood out behind like the rudder of a great ship.

Suppose the monster swam away with Roger still imprisoned? After he had used up the last air in his scuba tank, he would die.

Hal inserted the blade of his knife between the shark's lips and tried to pry them open. They did not budge.

In the meantime, Roger's eyes had grown accustomed to the darkness of his prison. The place was not as dark as a pocket after all. There was a very faint glimmer of light, possibly a phosphorescence from the tissues of the monster's mouth. No, it was not quite like that. It was more like daylight, but very faint. The boy told himself it was probably just his imagination. There couldn't be any daylight inside a fish's mouth.

Roger grinned when he thought how worried his brother must be. Why should he worry? There was nothing to worry about. He, Roger, was sitting there as snug as a bug in a rug. He hadn't a care in the world.

He thought differently when his air suddenly gave out. He sucked hard but got nothing. But there was a reserve supply. He flipped a switch and turned it on. It was a relief to be able to breathe again, but he knew the reserve was timed to last only five minutes.

So he had better open the door and get out. He tried, but the door was locked. He put his shoulders against the upper jaw and his feet against the lower and strained to force them apart. The only result was that he breathed faster, and at this rate would exhaust his air supply in less than five minutes.

He sat down again to think things over. There was still that faint light, even though the lips were firmly closed. He tried to find its source. It didn't come from the roof of the mouth nor from the floor. It seemed to come from the sides. And there it appeared to be in ridges, like the bars in a jail window. What could make these vertical streaks of light?

He ran his hand along the side of the mouth.

He found strips like the strings of a harp—or perhaps they were more like rubber bands, for they stretched. Each one when pressed aside let in more light, then closed again as his fingers left it. There seemed to be about five of them.

Gills! They must be gills. Every fish had them—must have them or quit breathing. They were part of the mechanism that enabled the fish to extract oxygen from the water. Scientists were already working on the problem of supplying man with artificial gills so that he could breathe like a fish below the sea. Perhaps ten, a hundred, a thousand years from now man could live and breathe underwater without an aqualung.

The question suddenly occurred to the boy, why hadn't the big fish swallowed him? There was probably room for half a dozen like him in that big stomach. Perhaps the fish was already full of food and was holding him in reserve until it was hungry. Or perhaps he tasted bad. Possibly the whale shark preferred shrimp and those other even smaller animal and plant organisms that floated everywhere. Anyhow, he was glad he was unpopular.

He thought again about the gills. He remembered a report made by James Dugan, famous diver who had worked for years with Cousteau. Dugan knew a fifty-year-old native of the Palau Islands who had been engulfed by a grouper. He made his escape through the gills.

A grouper, though a large fish, was small compared with the whale shark, and if a man could get out through a grouper's gills, it should be possible through the gills of this monster. He would try it. Otherwise he was slated to die within a few minutes.

He pressed the elastic gills apart and stuck his head out. He saw his brother's foot; the rest of him was on the other side of the fish trying to open the mouth.

Even with death so close, Roger's mischievous mind suggested that he play a trick on his brother. He might as well have some fun during his last three minutes.

He squeezed out between the rubbery gills. Keeping the fish between him and Hal, he swam to the jeep and crawled inside. He didn't need the scuba tank now. The same air mixture that had filled the tank filled the glass bubble. He took out the mouthpiece, removed the mask, and breathed deeply. He grinned with satisfaction, and settled himself comfortably to watch his brother.

Hal had brought out a hammer and was beating the closed lips. The big fish seemed to enjoy it. It appeared to wag its tail like a dog. Hal got a piece of stone-hard coral from a ledge and vigorously scratched the hide near the mouth. The only result was that the coral suffered more than the hide. The sandpaper armor of the fish pulverized the rock, and a shower of coral fragments drifted down through the water.

He resorted to gentler tactics. He stroked the monster

under the chin as he had seen Roger do. The big dog accepted this petting without opening its mouth one crack.

A cloud of little nothings drifted past the shark's nose. The monster opened its great mouth wide and the cloud was sucked in. Hal could see clear to the back of the cavern and there was nothing there. The fish must have swallowed Roger, tank and all.

Hal swam below and attacked the living submarine with his knife. His brother was probably dead, Hal thought, but perhaps he could at least get his body and give it decent burial. Otherwise, the gastric juices would soon digest the flesh and nothing would be left but the skeleton to ride the seas in this living tomb.

Hal had thought of the laser to kill the fish. But a beam of sufficient power to kill such a monster would certainly kill Roger too—if he were still alive. And he was probably as dead as a doornail already.

The skin on the belly was softer than any other part of the hide, but the knife, used with all the power of Hal's strong arm, did not even scratch it. He knew that he was only dulling his knife.

The big shark had had about enough of this tomfoolery. With a sweep of its great tail it swam away.

Hal swam back to the jeep, determined to turn on all power and pursue that shark to the ends of the Pacific if necessary. He crawled up into the jeep. He turned and saw Roger, sitting at ease and chewing a sea biscuit.

"How did you get here?" Hal demanded.

"Oh, I got tired of it out there so I came in. Where were you?"

"Never mind where I was. But wait until we get back to the house and I'll spank you within an inch of your life."

The Avalanche

The strangest job yet of the young naturalists was to hunt for water underwater.

Dr. Dick called them to his office. "We've had an accident," he said. "The desalting plant that turns salt water into fresh for drinking has broken down. We can't possibly bring in enough water by ship to supply the town. We're appealing to you to do something about it."

"Why us?" Hal asked. "What can we do?"

"We picked on you because you are the food men. You have been very successful in showing how the sea can supply more food than it ever has in the past. We believe you can make the sea produce fresh drinking water."

Hal laughed. "Do you think we are magicians? We found ways to get more food from the sea because it was right there waiting to be taken. But there's no fresh water in the ocean."

"That's where you're wrong," Dr. Dick said. "There are places where springs of fresh water come up through the sea floor. In the Hawaiian islands divers discovered water twelve degrees colder than the water around it. They tasted it and found it was fresh. They drank it, and there was no taste of salt. It was pouring up through the sea bottom. In the Mediterranean the town of Cassis near Marseilles ran short of water. Scientists discovered good water welling up from the sea bottom at the base of a cliff. Rainwater that fell on the top of the cliff was soaking down to the bottom where it struck a layer of hard rock and was forced to come up into the sea. The water was piped to the town and Cassis never again suffered a water shortage. We have a cliff right here, the precipice of the Great Barrier Reef. It is made of porous coral, and rain that falls on top of it must sink far down. Possibly it comes up again somewhere near the foot of the cliff. I suggest you explore a bit and see if you can find it."

Hal's eyes glowed with excitement. "It's a marvelous idea," he said. "Not just for this town, but all over the world."

"You catch on quickly," said Dr. Dick. "You can see what it would do for many dry parts of the world if they could get a constant flow of sweet water pouring in from the sea. Right here, Australia is a good example. Much of the land is desert. Crops won't grow. The soil is all right, but too dry. It needs water. Not salt water—that would ruin the soil. Salt water turned into fresh would be too expensive to use for irrigation. But fresh water piped from the sea could turn bare wastes into rich gardens and farms. There would be no cost except for the pipe. No pumps would be necessary, no costly desalting plants. Think what could happen in the Sahara, the Kalahari Desert, the Gobi, the American deserts. Of course all that is a long way off, but you would be one of the pioneers in something that could be mighty important in the future."

With their glass jeep anchored near the precipice, Hal and Roger went out on this fantastic search for fresh water in salt water. Foot by foot they explored the sea bottom at the base of the cliff. They stopped now and then, removed their mouthpieces, and tasted the water. It was salty.

They were about to go home for lunch when they heard a rumbling sound above. They looked up to see a great avalanche of rocks and coral blocks pouring down the face of the cliff. It was headed straight for them, and there was very little time to get out of the way. You cannot move rapidly underwater, especially at such a depth where the water is thick and heavy and makes going slow.

For a moment they froze with surprise and fright. Then Hal seized Roger's arm and pulled him into a cave in the cliff.

The landslide thundered down in front of the cave. It could do them no harm now—so they thought. The cave entrance was only four feet high and protected them perfectly.

But the rocks piled up until the opening was completely closed. Their place of refuge suddenly became a prison. The rumbling stopped. Now they could dig their way out.

But they had nothing to dig with. With their bare hands they tried to push away the great chunks of coral, some as big as their glass jeep. The sharp coral edges cut into their hands and they could feel the sticky blood that oozed out. They hoped the coral was dead—living coral could be very poisonous.

They shivered with cold. Why was this water so much colder than the water outside?

They must get out soon; their air was running low. Ten or fifteen minutes more and they would suffocate like drowned kittens. They went at the rocks again with new vigor. The harder they worked, the faster they used up their air.

It was like battling a stone wall. Except that a wall wouldn't have all these knives to bloody the hands.

They stopped to rest for a moment. But when they were not working, they got colder. Here they were in the tropical coral sea close to the equator, and the chill of this water was a mystery.

It was Roger this time who guessed the answer to the mystery. He remembered what Dr. Dick had said about the low temperature of springwater.

He took out his mouthpiece and tasted the water. It was fresh.

In the pitch-dark cave he searched for and found his brother's arm. He gave it a tug. Hal brushed his hand away. Roger felt for Hal's mouthpiece and yanked it out of his mouth.

Hal could not help gulping water, and one gulp was enough to tell him that they had found what they had been looking for. Now he was conscious of an upward pressure under his feet. That must be the fresh water welling up from beneath. The pressure was powerful, like the force of water from a fire hydrant.

He felt as if he were going down from a two-hundred-foot level to three hundred or perhaps four hundred. This must be because the water pouring in was unable to get out and pressed harder against the body just as it would at a hundred or more feet lower down.

This couldn't go on. Either the incoming flood would be choked to a standstill or, if it was stronger than the dam, the dam must break.

He let the pressure build up a little further. Then he fished around for Roger's hands, found them, and placed them against one of the biggest chunks of coral that blocked the opening.

Roger got the idea. Both boys pressed with all their strength. Their push combined with the pressure of the incoming springwater was enough to move the block about half an inch. A crack was opened and a little light filtered in.

Again they pushed and the big mass suddenly fell out, leaving a large-enough gap so that they could crawl through to freedom.

What had caused the avalanche? They peered up the face of the cliff. They could not quite see the top because it was above the surface. But there was a moving shadow up there that might be the shadow of a man. There was no way to guess who it could be.

They returned to the jeep and drove at once to the office of Dr. Dick.

"We found a spring," Hal reported. "It's good and strong and perfectly fresh. It's in a cave at the base of the reef."

"Wonderful," exclaimed Dr. Dick. He turned to the telephone. "I'll get the chief engineer and you can guide him to the spot. He and his crew will pipe the water into town and connect it up with our water system so every house will be supplied. I don't know whether you realize what a big thing this is. It means that from now on we won't need the desalting plant and that will save a lot of money. But it means a lot more than that. The Great Barrier Reef is 1,250 miles long and if there is a good spring here there must be hundreds more, enough to bring millions of acres of the wastelands of Australia into cultivation—and the same thing can be done elsewhere in the world. Did you have any difficulty in finding it?"

"Well, yes. We had a little brush with an avalanche. But without the avalanche we probably wouldn't have discovered the spring. We crawled into this cave to escape the landslide. Then Roger discovered that the water was fresh."

Dr. Dick looked puzzled. "Landslide? Coral formations aren't in the habit of sliding. It must have come down from the top. There's a lot of loose stuff on top of the reef, but I don't see how it could fall unless someone pushed it over the edge. But who could possibly have done that? Surely there isn't anybody in Undersea City who'd want to bury you."

Now was the chance to tattle to Dr. Dick about two men who might like very much to bury them. But suppose neither of those men was guilty. To cast suspicion on Oscar Roach would not be fair. It might lose him his job. And if they mentioned Kaggs, they would have to tell why he had it in for them—because they knew too much about his prison record and his murders. If it was true that he had reformed, he deserved a chance to make good.

The chief engineer arrived. They jeeped him to the cave. When he came back to the jeep, he said, "You must have had a rough time of it. Bad luck to be caught in there—you could have died like rats in a trap. The spring is great. Enough water to supply half a dozen towns the size of Undersea City. You were lucky to find it."

"You used the right word," Hal said. "Lucky. And if we hadn't had the bad luck, we wouldn't have had the good luck."

They returned to town and let the chief out at his office. Jeeping down Main Street, they caught sight of Oscar Roach just entering the hotel where he had his dishwashing job. Arriving home, they found Kaggs sitting in the living room reading his Bible. He looked up, and seemed surprised. "Didn't expect you back so soon," he said.

Bottom of the World

The telephone rang. Dr. Dick's voice was excited.

"We're planning something pretty special," he said. "Thought you might be interested. Can you come over?"

They swam down Barracuda and around the corner into Research Street to Dick's office.

"We want to do some exploring for minerals farther down," he said. "Would you like to go clear to the bottom of the deepest hole on earth?"

The proposition was so startling that the boys could only look at him with popping eyes.

"We've hired *Deepboat*," Dr. Dick explained. "You know, the bathyscaphe something like the *Trieste* that carried Jacques Piccard and Lieutenant Don Walsh to the deepest hole in the deepest ocean."

"You mean the Challenger Deep?" asked Hal.

Dr. Dick smiled. "I see you've heard of it."

"I read Piccard's story about it in his book *Seven Miles Down.* But that dive was made back in 1960. Hasn't anybody made it since then?"

"No one, up to now. The challenge still waits for somebody else. The Challenger Deep is a terrific canyon at the south end of the Mariana Trench in the Mariana Islands. You'll find Mariana Trench on the *National Geographic* map. It's a gorge seven times as deep as the Grand Canyon. Looking for minerals is not your job. But we thought you might like to go down to see what animal life, if any, there is down there. Some scientists say there can't be because the tremendous pressure would squeeze any fish to death. Others say it may be the home of monsters—creatures bigger than man has ever seen. Would you like to find out?"

"We certainly would," Hal said. "When do we start?"

"Our ship will leave tomorrow morning."

"But if we go up to the *Discovery*, we will get the bends," Hal said.

"That's not the ship," said Dr. Dick. "You'll go by hover-sub."

"Now you've got me. What's a hoversub?" Hal asked.

"You know the hovercraft—the boat that floats on a cushion of air twelve feet above the water. The British already have one whooshing back and forth across the Channel from England to France at seventy miles an hour. They're building five more. The United States is building some. It's called a hovercraft because it can hover or float in the air like a helicopter. And it can shoot along so fast because it doesn't have to fight the waves—just rides above them."

"But," said Hal, "if we go up to board the hovercraft, we get the bends just the same."

"That's where the hoversub comes in. It's so new it hasn't made the dictionary yet. The hoversub is a combination of hovercraft and submarine. It can travel underwater, though not very fast because the drag of the water holds it back; it can go much faster through the air. You can board it down here two hundred feet below. The air in it will be exactly the same as what you are breathing now—mostly helium. The cabin will be sealed tight so the air won't change. The hover-sub will rise above the waves and make the two-thousand-mile trip to the Marianas. Then it will sink again and meet *Deepboat* two hundred feet down. *Deepboat* will be charged with the same air, and will take you to the bottom and back without any change in pressure."

"Wonderful," Hal said, "if it works."

"Well," said Dr. Dick cheerfully, "if it doesn't work, you won't know it—because you'll be dead."

The boys laughed, but they thought it was pretty grim humor.

The next morning the hoversub was waiting at the corner of Research Street and Main. At the back it had jets like those of an airplane. On its belly was a great superjet from which air could be expelled with enough force to lift the vessel above the surface of the sea.

The boys crawled in through the open hatch. Already aboard were two geologists and the pilot. The geologists shook hands. They were young men, perhaps in their twenties, and seemed as highly excited as the two naturalists.

The hatch was sealed tight and the jets turned on. The hoversub climbed the two hundred feet to the surface and then burst through into the air as if it belonged there. It scudded along twelve feet above the waves.

"This thing must weigh a ton," Hal said. "Must be a pretty powerful motor to lift it this high."

"They say it's 3,500 horsepower," said one of the geologists. "How smoothly it rides! No pitching, no rolling. I like that. I get mighty seasick in an ordinary boat."

The sea was very choppy, but the crests of the waves never touched the flying submarine. They snarled and spit as if they were angry not to be able to toss this thing around as they could a surface craft of the same size. A fishing boat going in the same direction had a hard time bucking the strong wind and contrary waves. It was not making more than five miles an hour. The hoversub shot by it at seventy and there was scarcely time for the fishermen to wave before it was gone.

Even at this speed it would take sixty hours to get to the Marianas. So everybody settled down to sleep, or eat, or talk. The pilot put the controls on automatic and came back to join the others.

"This is slow coach compared with what they are planning," he said. "Ships that will weigh forty thousand tons and scoot just above the surface of the Atlantic and Pacific Oceans at speeds of several hundred miles an hour."

He sighted a coral reef lying dead ahead. It was about half a mile wide and three miles long. The pilot didn't even go back to the controls.

"Aren't you going to go around it?" Hal said anxiously.

"Don't need to," the pilot said. "Nothing to stop us there. No trees. Watch this bucking bronco get over it."

Hal and Roger watched nervously. The beach slanted up in a sloping bank. Surely the hoversub would strike the bank.

Instead, it rose as the bank rose and flew twelve feet above the land just as it had above the water. It sped across like a scared cat and slid down as the other shore sloped to sea level. And the pilot had not touched the controls.

One bare coral island after another was crossed in the same way. Only where there were coconut palms growing did the pilot have to go forward and guide the ship through the trees.

"It will go over swamps, bogs, marshes, or rivers in the same way," he said. "It will even climb a hill and go down the other side."

"Like riding a magic carpet," Roger said.

Magic carpet. It sounded good. So the men named the flying sub *Magic Carpet.*

"We'll be over an open stretch now," said the pilot. "So I think I'll take a nap. I'll have to be at the controls all night."

"But don't you need somebody up there while you're napping?" Hal asked.

"No, I don't think so. There are no more islands. Still, a ship might get in our way. Then the automatic wouldn't know what to do. I'll show you the controls so that you can take over in case of emergency."

It was very simple. Just one lever steered the craft right or left, up or down.

The pilot went back and was soon sound asleep. Hal took his seat behind the controls. He did not dare go off and leave everything to the automatic.

He studied the chart. They were over the open northern waters of the Coral Sea. He measured the distance against the speed of the craft. It would take about eight hours before the *Magic Carpet* could reach the island world of the Solomons and New Guinea. Then he would wake the pilot.

It was well along in the afternoon before he sighted the islands. The pilot was still asleep. Why rouse him? The tip of New Guinea pointed at him like a warning finger on the left. It would be easy enough to steer past it. Then there was a large gap between New Ireland and Bougainville. Anyone who couldn't find his way through here would be pretty stupid. And if any ship appeared, he could certainly go around it.

But he didn't reckon on two ships, popping out from behind two islands at the same time and about to pass each other directly ahead of him. He couldn't steer either to port or to starboard without hitting one of them. He could have stopped this contraption if he knew how, but the pilot had not shown him the position of the throttle. There was no time to call the pilot. Both islands were heavily forested and the *Magic Carpet* was not designed to go over forests.

A gap suddenly appeared between the trees on the starboard point. Perhaps he could hop the island there.

As he neared the shore he saw that the hopping was not going to be easy. The beach was not a gentle slope as it had been on the coral islands. In fact, there was no beach. The surf boiled against an overhanging bank. How high it was he couldn't be sure, but he was afraid it would be too high for the flying sub. If he plunged into the rocky wall below the overhang at seventy miles an hour, there would be no more *Magic Carpet* and no life left in its passengers.

Perhaps he could rise above it. He threw the steering lever into the up position. The hoversub did not rise. He had forgotten that this was not an airplane. It would go up through water because its jets kept pushing against the water. It could ride a cushion of air over land because the big jet blowing against the ground held it up. But twelve feet up was the limit.

Hal held his breath. He wanted to close his eyes so he couldn't see what happened. He thought of leaving the controls and rushing back to the rear of the cabin so he wouldn't get the full force of the crash. But he kept his eyes open and held on.

He expected to hear some cries of alarm behind him. He glanced back. All the others were sound asleep.

The hoversub struck the bank. It shuddered, but kept going. It plowed through the top layer of stones and dirt. It was crawling on its stomach. Would it make it or not? If it could just get its big jet over the ground, it would be pushed up into the air.

Then suddenly he knew it was all right. The powerful jet got its mouth over the edge of the bank and at once bounced the flying sub twelve feet up. The jolt made the pilot grunt and turn over in his sleep. The others seemed dead and did not know how near they had come to being really dead. Hal breathed a deep sigh of relief. He felt as if all his troubles were over. Nothing as bad as that could happen again.

Then he saw something else as bad as that straight ahead. A house was in his way and there was no time to go around it. The hoversub tore into the thatch roof, ripped a big hole in it, and passed through. Bits of thatch flew in every direction. The people in the house must have thought the end of the world had come. They burst out of the doors and windows, screaming.

One of them had a gun and took a potshot at the flying devil. He missed. Hal's passengers did not hear the shot over the roar of the flying sub's own engine.

But other natives heard it and ran out of their houses with guns, assuming that some enemy tribe was making war on them.

They fired at the hoversub and the bullets rattled on the fuselage. This could be serious. If they managed to make holes through the metal shell or smash a window, the high-pressure helium would pour out, low-pressure air would pour in, and everybody on board would die of the bends.

Luckily the shell, built to resist great water pressure, resisted the bullets while the Plexiglas bent like rubber but did not break.

A crowd of natives directly in the way scattered with shrieks of terror to both sides, not realizing that even those six feet tall would still be six feet below the flying monster. Some threw themselves flat on the ground and gave themselves up for dead. They were doubtless surprised to be still alive after the thing had passed.

Here was something they would remember the rest of their lives. The story would grow and grow. And someday the old men would take their grandchildren on their knees and tell them about the frightful dragon as big as the island spouting flame from its great red eyes and burning wind from a hole in its stomach, sweeping the land like a typhoon, killing thousands upon thousands of men, women, and children.

As a matter of fact, not a soul was hurt except perhaps a few who got bullets in their legs because the gunmen were too excited to shoot straight.

Seven Miles Deep

Another thrill waited for Hal at the other side of the island.

The sea here was very rough. Great billows dashed against the rocks, sending up fountains of spray. But what bothered Hal the most was that this bank was about twenty feet high. What would happen when the flying sub went over the edge?

The boat shot out into space. Now it was where it didn't belong, twenty feet above sea level. Its jet blast could not support it at this level. It dropped so heavily that it did not stop at twelve feet but went on down and plowed into the sea. A big fish lying in its path got out of the way with a powerful flick of its tail. The sub came out into the trough of a wave and was almost at once buried in another billow.

Then it began to gain altitude and in the next trough managed to climb to its proper height of a dozen feet.

Its driver had had enough. He put the controls on automatic and went back to give the pilot a good poke. That gentleman woke, blinking.

"Oh, it's you. I thought you were going to let me snooze until we got to the islands."

"We're past the islands," Hal said. He led the sleepy pilot forward and put his finger on the chart. "We're here, just beyond the Solomons."

"How did it go?" the pilot asked.

"Fine."

"No trouble?"

"No trouble."

"You were lucky."

"We're all lucky," Hal said. "Lucky to be alive."

The little ship flew on, day and night, past wonderful Truk embracing three hundred islets inside its coral reef, on to the south end of the Mariana Trench. There the pilot located *Deepboat* by radiotelephone and dove down two hundred feet to meet it. The two boats rubbed elbows.

The pilot of *Deepboat* dropped out of the open hatch, and the hatch of *Magic Carpet* was opened to receive him.

After introductions, he explained, "There isn't room in *Deepboat* for more than two men. I suppose you two naturalists will want to go down together, and you two geologists will wish to go down together. So that leaves me out. But you won't need me. *Deepboat* is not hard to operate. If one of you will go over with me now, I'll show you how to work it."

Hal insisted that the geologists have the first dive. One went with the pilot who showed him the controls. Then the pilot returned to *Magic Carpet,* and the other geologist joined the first. They closed the hatch, and *Deepboat* began to descend into the depths. Hal and Roger waited as patiently as they could for its return.

"By the way," Hal said, "why is it called *Deepboat?*"

The pilot replied, "Piccard, the man who invented the deep-diving boat, called it a bathyscaphe. *Bathys* is Greek for deep and *skaphē* is Greek for boat. But the builder of this one didn't see why English-speaking people should talk Greek.

So he just turned these words into English, and you have *Deepboat.*"

"Was it right here that Piccard's boat made its dive?"

"Right here. You are directly above the deepest hole that has ever been found in any ocean. It's called the Challenger Deep and, believe me, it's deep. Seven miles straight down."

"Did Piccard's boat go down all the way?"

"Clear to the bottom."

"Was his boat the same as *Deepboat*?"

"No. Not quite. His boat, called the *Trieste*, was much larger than *Deepboat* and heavier."

"Has *Deepboat* been down?"

"Only about a mile."

This was a surprise to Hal. He looked worried. "So if we four go deeper, we'll be testing it out for the first time."

"That's right," grinned the pilot. "Whatever you do will be at your own risk. The boat is designed to stand great pressure. But, who knows, it may cave in like an egg. And you'll come up as flat as pancakes."

This seemed to amuse him, but it didn't amuse Hal and Roger. "It doesn't seem to worry you," Hal said.

"Why should I worry?" the pilot answered. "It's none of my business. I was just told to bring it here and have it ready. It's ready. Of course if the geologists never come back, you won't need to go down. That's a happy thought."

This fellow, Hal reflected, is just too happy for any good use.

He breathed easier when, after an hour, *Deepboat* returned. It was still in good shape. The two geologists came back to *Magic Carpet.*

"How did it go?" Hal asked.

"Very well. We studied the rock strata all the way down the face of the canyon."

"All the way? You went to the bottom?"

"Oh, no. That wasn't necessary. We went down about two miles. We learned all we needed to, so there was no reason for going farther."

"Now it's your turn," said the happy pilot of *Deepboat*, and took Hal over to show him the controls. The pilot returned in a few moments and Roger went over to join Hal. They made the hatch tight, then turned on the top jets that would push the craft down into the depths of the sea.

There was still some daylight, but it faded rapidly as they went deeper. Soon it was as dark as night.

The pilot had been right, the thing was too small for more than two men. Even for two it was a tight fit. It seemed to be a perfectly round steel ball. Through its Plexiglas windows they could see the stars of this underwater night. But these stars were all racing about madly.

The stars were of all colors, red, yellow, green, blue, lavender . . . They were the lights carried by the phosphorescent fish.

A lantern fish went by, a row of lights down each side like the portholes of a ship. Shrimp threw out bright flames. Jellyfish glowed softly. Venus's-girdles were outlined as with neon tubes.

The hatchetfish was equipped with indirect lighting. The "deep-sea dragon" was conspicuous with its rows of green and blue lamps. The graybeard sported illuminated whiskers.

Squid peered out of eyes rimmed with lights, and more lights dotted their tentacles. Toadfish showed no lights when their huge mouths were shut; but when open, a string of lights like a necklace of pearls appeared along the base of the teeth.

All these creatures lived far down beyond the reach of daylight, hence their need of lights. Why some of the lights were white, some yellow, some red, some blue, some green, science had not explained.

One carried what looked like a small electric bulb suspended from a sort of fishing pole in front of its face. This attracted smaller fish. Then the light was jerked out of the way and the little fish found themselves between the jaws of the fisherman.

The moon rose. At least it looked like the moon, but Hal said it was a moonfish. It was perfectly round, a full ten feet in diameter, flat and thin, and glowed like the moon.

It is also called the headfish, since it appears to be nothing but head. When young it has a tail, but drops it as a tadpole does. What looks like only a head actually contains the stomach and other organs. On the edge of the big moon are two small eyes. Tiny, almost invisible fins along the moon's edge propel the ton-weight of the huge fish slowly through the water.

A curious thing about the phosphorescent fish was that they left trails of phosphorescence behind them, like the tails of meteors.

A fairly large fish was sprinkled all over with lights.

"They call it the star eater," Hal said. Even its fins were illuminated. From its chin dangled brilliantly lighted whiskers.

"But there's one without any lights," Roger said. "Why is that?"

"It's called the blindfish," Hal said. "It's totally blind, so it couldn't use lights to see where it is going. It just moves along slowly like a blind man walking down the street tapping his cane ahead of him. Only in this case there are about twenty canes—those long feelers that spread out in every direction. With these the fish can feel its way along and find its food."

"How deep are we now?" Roger asked.

Hal looked at the illuminated depth gauge. "Eighteen hundred fathoms. Let's see—a fathom is six feet. So we're down about two miles."

"That's as far as the geologists went," Roger said. "Do we go up now?"

"Not a chance," Hal said. "They had good reason for going up—they had seen all they wanted to. But we haven't begun to see what we came here to see. We want to find out what there is at the bottom—monsters, or no life at all?"

"Didn't Piccard and his pal find out?"

"They thought they saw a flatfish and some shrimp. Other scientists say they must have been mistaken—that no fish could stand the terrific pressure. Perhaps we'll find out who was right."

"But we'll be the first to go down that far in *Deepboat*," Roger said. "Aren't you afraid?"

"Of course I am," Hal admitted. "But someone has to test out this thing and we may as well be the ones. Until it begins to buckle in on us, we'll keep going down."

Deepboat bumped hard and stopped.

"We must be at the bottom already," said Roger. "Or else we struck a big fish."

"No," Hal said. "We bumped into a thermocline."

"What's a thermocline?"

"Look out the window," said Hal. "See what looks like a floor?"

The thousands of small illuminated sea creatures lying on it did make it look like a floor.

"That's a thermocline," Hal said. "The ocean isn't the same all the way down. It comes in layers like a layer cake. The top layer is warm water. The thermocline divides the warm water above from the colder water below. You noticed how we bounced up when we hit it. It's a sort of heavy elastic sheet like the one a circus performer bounces on when he falls from a trapeze."

"Can we get through it?"

"Sure." Hal turned on a little more power. *Deepboat* struck the thermocline again, broke through, and continued down.

Twice more they struck thermoclines, bounced up a few yards, put on more power, and got through.

Suddenly everything in the sea began to rush upward at a great rate. Hal turned on the searchlight. The canyon wall beside them was flying up at great speed.

"What's going on now?" Roger worried. "I didn't know so many things could happen on a deep dive."

Hal looked at the tachometer. It measured their diving rate. "We're going down twice as fast as we should. We've been caught in a current going down this cliff. It's a sort of river in the ocean—but a strange river because it goes straight down rather than on the level." He turned off the engine. "We don't need any power now," he said. "We get a free ride."

The free ride did not last long. The swift drop ended in a sickening crash. There was no bounce this time. They had really struck something hard. *Deepboat* stopped dead.

"I hope that didn't crack open a seam somewhere," said Hal, inspecting the inside wall of their little prison. "I don't see any water coming in."

"What happened?"

"Struck a ledge sticking out from the cliff. If we can't get off it, our trip ends right here. I'll try going up a little."

Deepboat did not budge. The force of the torrent coming from above held it firmly to the ledge.

This was a pretty pass. They couldn't go either up or down.

"We'll try going sideways," Hal said. He diverted the power to the side jets. The boat began to roll toward the edge. The boys found themselves upside down. With a great deal of scraping and grinding, *Deepboat* reached the edge and dropped off. It righted itself, much to the relief of its passengers, and then continued its swift descent.

This went on for another thousand feet. Then the torrent

mysteriously faded away like a river in the desert sinking into the sand.

No sooner had the trippers to the bottom of the world begun to breathe easily than their craft struck again. But this strike was quite different. It was not a hard jolt, but soft and squashy.

"Another thermocline?" said Roger.

"Perhaps," Hal said. He put on more power. If this was another thermocline, he could break through it. But *Deepboat* did not move.

"Perhaps we've reached the bottom," Roger said.

Hal looked at the depth gauge. "Nowhere near it yet," he answered.

"Then what can be holding us up?"

"I don't know," Hal confessed.

"Look!" cried Roger. Something had come up where the searchlight could shine upon it. What looked like two enormous eyes were visible through the window.

"They can't be eyes," Hal said. "Nothing has eyes as big as those. They look as big as a ship's portholes."

The great eyes looked like pools of angry green, lit from the inside.

"Perhaps it's a giant octopus," Roger guessed.

"No," Hal said. "Even the biggest octopus has small eyes. And they don't glow like these. These seem to be phosphorescent."

Something like a huge snake passed across the window.

Hal exclaimed, "Now I know what it is. The cousin of the giant octopus. The supergiant squid. It's ten times the size of a big octopus."

"How large do you suppose this one is?" Roger asked.

"Judging by the size of those eyes," Hal said, "and the size of that tentacle we just saw, I'd guess it might be fifty or sixty feet long."

Roger whistled. "What a monster! It's a good thing it's not dangerous."

"Not dangerous!" exclaimed Hal. "Guess again. People over here call it the nightmare of the Pacific. Another common name for it is devilfish. Luckily it's very seldom seen because it prefers to stay far down. There's that tentacle again. Look at the big cups on it."

"Like the cups of an octopus," said Roger.

"Yes, but quite different. The cups on the tentacle of an octopus are for hanging on. They are suction cups. The squid's cups are for killing." He directed the searchlight into one of the cups. It was lined with big sharp teeth. "Anything or anybody that gets caught by those cups is dead before it gets to the squid's mouth. And the mouth is even more dangerous. Let's see if we can find it." He moved the searchlight down from the big eyes until it rested upon the animal's enormous beak.

"It looks as hard as iron," Roger said. "How could any animal with such a soft mushy body have such terrific jaws?"

"It could crush a shark with those jaws," Hal said. "Or split open your head as easily as you could crack a walnut."

Roger was impatient. "We can't stay here forever. Why doesn't it move along?"

"It's too much interested in us. It's probably wondering if it can crack this nut and get at us."

"Let's get out of here," Roger suggested. "If you can't push it down out of the way, why not lose it by going up a bit?"

"I'll try," said Hal. He turned on the lower jets. That should send the boat up. But *Deepboat* did not move.

"The beast must have one of its tentacles wrapped around over the top of the ball."

With its prey trying to escape, the animal became infuriated and threw other arms around *Deepboat*. Some of them almost covered the Plexiglas windows.

Roger was worried. "I think it's gripping us with all eight arms."

"All ten," Hal said. "Your old friend the octopus has eight arms—the squid has two more." Hal turned on every ounce of power.

The ball did not move. They could hear the great jaws grinding on the steel hull. The monster was fighting mad now. The sharp teeth in its tentacles were scraping over the hull.

Hal turned off the engine. "It's no use," he said. "We'll just have to wait."

The devilfish kept on biting and scratching. It had never encountered an enemy as tough as this one. The ball was too big to be swallowed whole and it didn't crack easily. The giant was becoming more and more irritated.

"It's getting on my nerves," Roger said.

"Don't worry. It can't get through solid steel."

But there was real cause for worry when the squid attacked one of the windows. Plexiglas was very tough, yet it was not steel. It could resist tremendous pressure. But it could be cut by something very sharp and the beak that was now pounding against it was very sharp.

Hal tried to estimate the size of the creature. It was about twelve feet around and must weigh at least a thousand pounds.

"There's one good thing," he said. "Even if he breaks that little window, he can't get in. He's much too big."

"I'm not afraid of his getting in," Roger said. "But if he makes just a little hole, the sea can get in and what happens then?"

Hal didn't like to terrify his young brother, but he must tell the truth. "In that case, I'm afraid it would be curtains for both of us. The water pressure must be at least a hundred times the air pressure in this ball. So the water would pour in at a tremendous rate and we would drown in a few minutes."

The squid's operations had attracted an audience. Fish of all sizes and shapes came up to watch what was going on. They were a rainbow of many colors in the glow of the searchlight.

Farther back there was something like a cloud passing through the water.

"What do you suppose it is?" wondered Roger. "It's too big to be a fish. Perhaps it's just a shadow."

The thing that looked like a great gray shadow came closer.

"I hope . . ." began Hal, but he didn't say what he hoped. He was disappointed when the shadow passed and was gone.

Presently it came back. Now it was squarely in the beam of the searchlight. It had an enormous block of a head as big as a bus. Its mouth was open and its huge teeth shone white.

"A sperm whale!" Hal exclaimed. "Perhaps it will help us out."

"What can it do?" Roger asked.

"It can save us from a watery death," said Hal, "if it takes a notion to do it. One of the sperm whale's favorite foods is squid. Not the little squid a foot or two long that swim near the surface, but the juicy giants that live far down. I only hope it's hungry."

The whale appeared again. It came within a few yards of the squid, then swam away.

"I'll bet it's afraid," Roger said.

"It has good reason to be. Many whales have been killed by squid."

"I should think it would always win," Roger said. "It's a lot bigger than the squid."

"Yes, but it doesn't have ten tentacles thirty feet long armed with thousands of teeth."

The whale drifted back and lay for a while watching its enemy with tiny eyes that contrasted oddly with the enormous hubcaps of the squid.

Then with a mighty thrust of its tail, it shot forward. Its mouth, as big as a door, opened to take in its favorite food. It would have this meal all to itself because no other creature would dare attack the giant squid. The whale's teeth looked as sharp as razors. They were no good for chewing, but could inflict a terrible bite.

The squid detached one arm from the steel ball and thrashed out against the approaching enemy. The whale snapped at the great snakelike tentacle and got it firmly between its teeth. Now it was teeth against teeth. When it came to teeth, the squid was a match for the whale. The hundreds of sharp points on the great arm must sink deep into the whale's enormous tongue, the most sensitive part of its entire body.

At once the whale spun about and made off, opening its mouth to get rid of this torture. But the squid did not let go. The result was a dizzy ride for the two passengers in *Deepboat*. They were being towed across the gorge with amazing speed. It was not a smooth ride. With every convulsive move of the whale in its effort to get free of the torturing arm, the ball bounced or rolled violently from one side to the other, tossing the boys against the walls until they were bruised and bloody.

Now they were getting near the other wall of the canyon. Their wobbling searchlight caught flashes of it, a straight up-and-down precipice of solid rock.

At the last moment the whale swung away from the cliff and the ball struck it with terrific force. The whirlabout had turned *Deepboat* upside down and the shock of striking the cliff while standing on their heads was so sharp that they almost passed out. Their big towboat now pulled them across toward the other cliff where they would probably get the same rough treatment.

But the whale, finding it could not shake the toothy arm loose from its tongue, closed its teeth upon it and bit it off. The sudden pain caused the squid to change color to an angry red. Now it took away its nine remaining arms from *Deepboat* and wrapped them around the head and over the eyes of the whale. All the sharp knives on the great arms sank into the whale's flesh, and blood turned the water pink.

But the whale was by no means beaten. Its head was tied up, but its mighty tail was still free. It could not reach its own head with its tail. With the intelligence of its cousin, the dolphin, it struck *Deepboat* a terrific blow and threw the hard steel ball up against the soft pulpy body of the squid.

The result was that the squid was turned into a pancake. It would soon round out again if left to itself; but the blow had also driven it up against the open jaws of the whale which promptly bit off a chunk of squid as big as a donkey.

That was too much for the giant of the deep. The whale dined on the remains of the dead squid at leisure, while the boys felt their bruises and collected their wits.

They were not only badly beaten up but very cold. The thermometer told them that the temperature was only two degrees above freezing.

"I suppose it will get colder and colder the farther down we go," Roger lamented.

It did seem to do just that until they finally broke through another thermocline.

"Now we're within a mile of the bottom," Hal said.

He studied the thermometer. "Seems to me it's getting a bit warmer," he said.

"How could that be?"

"I don't know. But I can guess. There may be volcanic fires

under the bottom. You know, the farther down you go in some mines, the hotter it gets. The subterranean heat beneath the floor of this trench may be warming up the bottom layer of water. Anyhow, there's no doubt about it—the mercury is climbing a bit."

Here was something new for Roger to worry about. Would they boil when they got to the bottom? Perhaps they would drop into an underwater volcano. He said as much to Hal.

"I don't think it will be that bad," Hal said. "Anyhow, we'll soon know." He watched the depth gauge. "Only thirty fathoms yet to go. Now only twenty. Now eighteen—fifteen—ten. Brace yourself—we may bump hard."

But there was no jolt. *Deepboat* settled down into something as soft as a feather bed. They were in mud almost up to the windows.

They had expected it to be icy cold down here. But the mercury had actually risen a little. It had climbed two degrees. That was not much, but enough to indicate that there was heat under this mud.

The mud that had clouded the water when they struck was settling now.

They peered out the windows. Here they were at the deepest known spot in all the oceans. The Grand Canyon was a mile deep. They had gone six miles deeper. They had gone down farther than Mt. Everest goes up. Everest was the highest mountain on the planet. Sir Edmund Hillary had climbed it. He reached the very top, 29,028 feet above sea level. Everybody thought that was a great accomplishment—and so it was. But two boys had now gone down 36,198 feet below sea level. In a few minutes they would climb again, 7,170 feet more than Hillary had climbed—but it would be much easier with the help of *Deepboat.* They had proved that this craft could stand the terrific pressure of the deep. It was as tough as Piccard's bathyscaphe.

Deepboat was more like a submarine than a bathyscaphe. No submarine had ever gone so far down. Perhaps builders of submarines would take advantage of what had been learned from this experiment and build subs that could go far deeper than a few hundred feet below the surface.

There was another thing they had not proved yet. Could life exist at this tremendous depth? Piccard had claimed that he saw animals on the bottom. He had taken photographs of them, but because of the cloudiness of the water the photographs when developed didn't show a thing. So nobody took his report very seriously. It was almost impossible to believe that any living thing could stand a pressure of two hundred thousand tons on its body.

"Look," cried Hal. "Isn't that thing moving?"

It was not just a cloud of mud. It was something alive. It rose from the bottom and swam slowly away. In a few minutes it returned bringing three others with it.

It was a flatfish, like a sole. It was about a foot long and half that across.

"See—it has two eyes on top of its head."

"I think there's something the matter with *your* head," said Roger. "You're dreaming—like Piccard."

"Look for yourself," said Hal.

Roger had to believe it. There were two wide-open eyes and they were on top of the head.

"All flatfish, like sole and skate, have both eyes on top," Hal reminded him.

"But why does it have eyes?" Roger objected. "If it weren't for that searchlight, it would be pitch-black down here. Animals that live where they don't need eyes lose their sight."

"That's what we've always thought," Hal agreed. "But you can see for yourself it's not true. Or at least, not always. I've got to take a picture of this."

He turned the full beam of the searchlight on the flatfish,

carefully read the exposure meter, and took several shots. His camera was of the instant developing sort and he could see his results within a few minutes. The flatfish showed up plainly.

"And what are those small things?" Roger said. "They look like red shrimp."

"That's exactly what they are," Hal said, and he took more pictures.

Little wriggly tracks showed that there must be more small animals beneath the mud.

"And there's a fish I've never seen before in all my life," said Hal.

It looked like a bad dream. It had a great savage mouth a foot wide armed with teeth that could easily grind hard-shelled crabs and lobsters to bits and could nip off a human arm at one bite. The mouth seemed to be about all there was to it. The rest of the body tapered down to a thin tail and was covered with what looked like feathers but must be an unusual form of scales. Hal took a photograph of it. Then he caught it between the jaws of the steel grab.

"What do you want it for?" Roger asked.

"I'll bet it's new to science," Hal said. "Of course it will die before we get it back to Undersea City. But then I'll put it in a jar of preservative and send it to a museum to be classified and named."

"What makes you think the scientists don't know about it already?" Roger asked.

"Of course I'm not sure," said Hal. "But I haven't seen the like of it in any manual. I think we've discovered a new species."

Roger was not easily convinced. "But most everything has already been discovered. We can't expect to find anything new."

"Why not?" said Hal. "New animals are being discovered

every year. Recently the Smithsonian Institution collected fish in the Marshall Islands. They got 481 species. Seventy-nine of them were new. That's one out of every six. Actually, human beings are only beginning to learn the mysteries of the ocean, and the very deep waters like these are practically unknown."

"Well," Roger said, "I have a name for this one already. *Nightmare huntii.*"

Hal laughed. *"Nightmare* is good. But I'm sure they won't give it our name. That's too much to expect. Let's go up."

At first they climbed very slowly. The thick, heavy water held them back. They did not mind—it gave them time to see what went on about them. Many times they were happy that they were protected by the steel ball.

A huge manta, or sea bat, as big as a barn door peered in one of the windows. It must have been twenty feet across from the tip of one wing to the tip of the other. And almost as long as it was wide.

The sea bat was not a man-eater. But still it could cause trouble. It could come up under a small boat and upset it. It could leap ten feet into the air, and if there happened to be a boat under it when it came down, its two-ton weight could smash the boat and kill the passengers. But though it had a mouth five feet wide, it had no taste for steel balls and could not have swallowed *Deepboat* if it had tried. It loved to play. It cavorted around the ball, gave it a push or two, then swam away.

"Look—a dragon!" exclaimed Roger. It certainly looked like one, and was quite terrifying as it came billowing into the beam of the searchlight. It was a full thirty feet long, not round, like a snake, but flattened and silver-sided, with a small mouth and deep-set, terrible eyes. But its most amazing feature was a flaming red mane like the mane of a horse that stood straight up from its head and neck. This waving mane did a sort of dance of fire in the unearthly submarine light. Two long spikes that looked as sharp as daggers projected from the back of the head.

Hal said, "Sailors who have spotted it swimming along the surface with its head out of the water have thought that they were looking at a sea serpent. Its real name is oarfish, because it is flattened like an oar. It rises to the surface at sunset, but spends the day at great depths like these."

The next passerby was an eighteen-foot stingaree. It was a bad-tempered fish, would attack anything that came in its way, and did promptly attack the steel ball. It covered it like a blanket and tried to sting it to death. It was disappointed. *Deepboat* continued to rise, but more slowly because of the weight of the monster.

"Wish we could get rid of this thing," Hal complained.

"Turn on your top jets," Roger suggested.

"Good idea," said Hal, and the stingaree found itself pushed up and away from the ball by the powerful jets.

It was a parade of monsters. The terror of the western Pacific, the great white shark, sometimes called White Death, most murderous of all sharks, a good forty feet long and equipped with many rows of saw-edged, razor-keen teeth, swam slowly by.

"See the barracuda," Hal said.

Roger examined the creature. "That's no barracuda," he said. "The barracuda never gets that big."

"There are seven species of barracuda," Hal said. "This one is called the great barracuda. People out here have another name for it, Tiger of the Sea. Most barracuda don't make trouble. But this one is always asking for it. Swimmers who have had their feet bitten off and don't know what struck them imagine it must have been a shark, but more often the villain is the Tiger.

"Now there's something really exciting," Hal exclaimed. "I must get a picture of that."

"Why, it's just a shark," said Roger.

"Yes, but it's a shark that has been dead for seventy million years."

"Then how come it's alive now?"

"It's the goblin shark," Hal said. "Its fossil remains have been found in many parts of the world. But no one has reported seeing a live one, so the scientists put it down as extinct. But there it is alive and well. It's only one of many creatures that naturalists have dismissed as being dead and gone, but are alive in some parts of the world, hidden away in the forests or in the deep waters of the ocean."

He took the creature's picture. That picture would make the authors of books on sea life add one more to the list of living creatures thought to have died out millions of years ago.

Arriving within two hundred feet of the surface, they used their phone to locate the *Magic Carpet*. They were glad to climb into the hoversub which was so much larger and more comfortable than the steel ball.

"How far down did you go?" one of the geologists asked.

"All the way," Hal said.

"Why all the way?"

"We were under orders. Dr. Dick wanted us to see what went on at the bottom."

"But we already know what goes on at the bottom," said the young geologist. "Nothing. Nothing could live under that pressure. Piccard took photographs down there. They didn't show a thing."

"Look at these pictures," Hal said.

The four flatfish could be plainly seen. Also the red shrimp.

And the feather-scaled creature, new to science, that Roger had named *Nightmare huntii.*

"Never would have believed it," said the pilot.

"But these are small things," said one of the geologists. "It looks as if the scientists who say that there may be monsters deep down are talking through their hats."

"Not quite," Hal said. "We saw a fight between a whale and a giant squid. We were visited by the dragon oarfish and a giant manta and the great white shark."

"And don't forget the stingaree," said Roger.

"And the goblin shark," Hal said. One of the geologists stared.

"You must have made a mistake," he said. "I've seen pictures of the fossils of the goblin shark. It died out millions of years ago."

"So we all thought," Hal agreed. "But look at this picture."

The three others studied the photograph with interest.

"Well, it seems to me," admitted one of the geologists, "you have a pretty good report to make to Dr. Dick."

St. George and the Dragon

Back in Undersea City, the boys went at their work with new energy.

They started fish farms where the best food fish could be grown, protected from sharks by those "undersea cowboys," the dolphins. They had lobsters from Maine flown in and started a lobster farm. The best oysters from New England were planted and would grow to full size in half the time it would take in the colder waters of the American coast or Japan. By placing tiny grains of sand within the shells in the Japanese fashion they could produce cultured pearls. They discovered a place where whales gathered, and conducted experiments in milking them, for whale's milk is a rich, nutritious food. Milking machines drew off the milk. One whale could produce a ton of milk a day. The milk was too rich to drink, but it was valuable in cooking and processing other foods.

The new fish they had found was sent in a bottle of preservative to the American Museum of Natural History by Dr. Dick, who insisted upon sending along Roger's name for it,

Nightmare huntii. The museum accepted the name, and the young naturalists were more pleased to have a fish named after them than they would have been to have a monument erected in their honor.

Dr. Dick called them in. "I have only one fault to find with you," he said.

"What is that?" Hal asked.

"You have neglected one of your two jobs."

"What two jobs?"

"One was to work for us. You've done that very well indeed. The other was to work for yourselves. You seem to have forgotten that. The understanding at the start was that besides serving the Undersea Science Foundation you were to be allowed to carry on your own work of collecting specimens for the aquariums of John Hunt and Sons. You'd better get on with that, or your father will be suing us for using up all of your time."

"But who will take our place?" Hal asked. "Oscar Roach?"

"If you think he can do it."

"I think so," Hal said. "I've been showing him the ropes, whenever I could get him away from his dishwashing. He'll make you a good naturalist."

At first Hal had mistrusted Roach and trusted Kaggs. Now he had grown to trust Roach, but was beginning to have his doubts about the "missionary."

Roach was delighted with his promotion from dishwasher to naturalist.

The boys turned to their second job. They collected rare specimens alive and transferred them to the tanks of the *Flying Cloud.* That ship would take them to Brisbane where they would be put aboard cargo vessels that would carry them to the Hunt Animal Farm on Long Island.

Their father would sell them to oceanariums such as Sea World near San Diego, Marineland near Los Angeles, the

Marineland of Florida, the aquarium at Honolulu, Hawaii's Sea Life Park, and dozens of similar institutions all over the world.

Three gorgeously colored triggerfish would be worth twelve hundred dollars. A very rare shark was caught. Australians had an odd name for it—the wobbegong. Elsewhere it is known as the carpet shark. When hauled up suddenly out of the sea, it bursts with a sound like a rifle shot. The first one the boys got exploded before Captain Ted could get it into a tank. Another was eased up more slowly so as not to excite it and was successfully tanked.

The hammerhead shark was a prize worth five hundred dollars because its head shaped like a hammer was the most unusual in the shark world.

When the tanks were full, Hal estimated the total value of the collection as coming very close to $100,000.

Dr. Dick came around to the Hunt home with bad news.

"I'm sorry to have to call on you for a little more help," he said. "A shark has been killing some of our people. It has done away with eight men during the last seven days. We have tried to frighten it away, but it seems to prefer to make its home in Undersea City. It swims up and down the streets, and when people see it coming they rush to take refuge in their houses. People are afraid to go to the stores to get food, workmen are afraid to go to work. The shark has things all its own way. It goes right on picking off one person after another, and there seems to be nothing we can do about it."

"Where do we come into it?" Hal asked.

"You know sharks. We don't. Our miners know mining, the merchants know selling, our police know ordinary police duties, your good friend the Reverend Mr. Kaggs knows the Bible, Roach is new to his job. Nobody has expert knowledge of sharks except you two. We want you to get rid of this unwelcome visitor before it kills any more of our people."

"What kind of shark is it?" Hal asked.

"I don't know. It's blue above and white below. Its body is slim and pointed. It has long gill slits. It's about twenty-five feet long and must weigh a ton. Most sharks hesitate to attack people but this one doesn't. It rushes in like a bolt of lightning. Sometimes it knocks a man down with its tail and then bites. Its teeth are very large and sharp. It takes off a leg or arm at one bite."

Roger looked at his brother. "It must be the mako," he said.

"Right," said Hal. "You've given us a very good description of it. It's the mako, and no mistake. Along this coast they call it the man-eater. It has terrible teeth. Weren't the teeth of your shark four inches long?"

Dr. Dick nodded.

"It's a meanie," Hal said. "Even when it's full of food it will attack—just because it's vicious by nature. I wish you had given us any other member of the shark family to deal with. We don't dare guarantee results, but we'll do what we can."

"That's all we can ask," said Dr. Dick. He seemed well satisfied that the boys would find some way to get rid of this killer.

After he had gone Roger said, "Let me do it."

Hal was surprised. "Of course, you can help me."

"No," Roger said. "You have other things to do. We can't stop all of our regular work just to fool around with a shark. I can do that alone."

"But this is no ordinary shark," Hal reminded him. "The mako is the toughest and meanest brute in the Coral Sea. A boy would be no match for it. It's a man's job."

Roger bristled. "And you think you're a man," he said.

"Don't forget, you're only five years older than I am."

Hal suddenly understood what his young brother was thinking. Roger wanted to do this thing to prove that he was not just a kid.

Reluctantly, Hal said, "All right. Go ahead and try."

"You don't think I can do it."

"I didn't say that. But if you find you need help, let me know."

Roger took the foot-long knife from his belt and began to sharpen the blade on a whetstone.

Hal looked on with amazement. "You're not going to tackle that shark with a knife!"

"Why not?"

"It would never get through the shark's hide."

"His underside is soft," Roger said.

"But you tried that once and it didn't work."

"I didn't try hard enough. If I have a good sharp knife and put some real power behind it, I think I can make him feel it."

Hal saw that it was useless to argue.

Roger slipped on his aqualung, mask, and flippers, and slid out through the hole in the floor. Where would he be most likely to find the mako? Where there were the most people. That would be on Main Street. He went down Barracuda, turned into Research Street, and stopped at the corner of Research and Main.

There were some people but no shark. The more venturesome miners were going to work, a few housewives were going to stores, young fellows who had no work were hanging around street corners just as they did in the world above. They couldn't whistle at the girls who went by, but attracted their attention by striking their scuba tanks with a stone or stick.

Small, brightly colored reef fish swam around the heads of

pedestrians, and there were a few larger fish, tuna, mackerel, and sea bass. Some people tried to grab them with their bare hands. One man succeeded and his family would have tuna for dinner.

Some sharks appeared but they were small and timid and certainly not man-eaters.

Then Roger saw the mako idling down the street. There was no mistaking it—it was blue above, white below, and its teeth were four inches long. It stared about through big eyes like lamps.

People vanished from the street as if by magic. They plunged into the nearest shops, houses, public buildings. Roger felt like doing the same. People peered out through glass windows. They signaled to him to take refuge. Roger thought it was a very good idea, but there was something within him that forced him to swim up toward the oncoming enemy.

He had read about shark hunters who frightened the shark by swimming straight at it. Roger tried it. He was almost paralyzed with fear. Those great lamp eyes seemed to grow larger and more menacing the closer they came. The mako did not show the slightest inclination to back down or turn away. Instead, it opened its jaws ready to receive this tasty breakfast. Its hundreds of teeth, five rows in the lower jaw and five in the upper, made the dental apparatus of a lion or tiger look like nothing at all.

A shark that had never before met a human might be timid. But this one had met and killed eight humans within a week and had found them easy picking. Roger saw almost too late that he was not going to bluff this monster. When he was two feet away from the terrible reception committee of bared teeth, he dived and slid along the shark's underside. He turned on his back and with all his strength drove the knife upward against the smooth white skin.

The knife slightly dented the hide but that was all. Then the shark was gone.

Roger thrust his knife into the holster and swam back to the house.

"How did you make out?" Hal asked.

"No luck. I jabbed him hard but the hide was too tough. I'm going to try a spear. After all, that's what St. George used against the dragon, and dragons are tougher than sharks."

He had always been fascinated by that old story. The dragon had been devouring humans and now was after the king's daughter. St. George had a soft spot in his heart for the princess and undertook to kill the dragon. He drove it through with his spear and he and the princess lived happily ever after.

Now it was the same thing over again except that the killer was a shark instead of a dragon and there was no princess.

Armed with a spear of the finest steel with a point as sharp as a needle, Roger sallied forth. But just in case the spear should fail, he carried an extra weapon—an underwater revolver.

People had left their shelters and were once more walking or swimming along Main Street. They panicked again when the great shark cast its shadow on the street. One pretty girl who did not move quickly enough was caught between the huge jaws and held to be eaten at leisure. She took the place of the princess in the old legend, and St. George Roger Hunt was here to save her.

This time he had no fear. His concern for the girl's life made him brave. He put all the power he could muster into the thrust of his sharp spear.

He did not even see a dent. He had done nothing but bend the point of his spear.

Disgusted, he dropped the spear and drew his revolver. He had read accounts of hunters who had fired at a shark only to have their bullets bounce back from the beast's armor plate. He didn't believe such stories. How could the toughest skin resist a bullet?

He fired. The bullet bounced back as if it had struck a steel spring. It struck Roger in the leaden weight belt. If it had landed an inch higher or an inch lower, it would have finished him off.

However, the bullet had disturbed the shark more than either the knife or the spear. It opened its jaws and dropped its prey. She lay crumpled up on the street. The mouthpiece of her aqualung had fallen from her lips and she would die within a few minutes for lack of air. Roger tried to replace the mouthpiece, but the unconscious girl could not hold it.

He looked wildly about for help. The shark was coming back. The nearest place of escape was the hatch of the hotel. Roger dragged her up through the opening onto the floor. Here she could breathe without the aqualung. She gradually revived, and was taken to another room to rest after her harrowing ordeal.

A baffled and humbled St. George looked out the hotel window at his victorious enemy which was nosing the glass on the other side. Roger didn't feel like St. George anymore. This was a tougher job than he had bargained for.

Then another idea came to him. He knew that the mako was an expert jumper. Makos have been known to leap out of the water ten or fifteen feet high. With their hatred of humans, they would sometimes make this tremendous jump just in order to fall down on a small boat, break it in two, and drown the passengers.

Sometimes the leap killed the mako. If it leaped near a beach, it was apt to fall on the beach and be unable to get back into the water. After wriggling about in vain it would die.

If he could make this mako jump—but there was no beach to land on. How about the hotel lobby? The "front door" in the floor was much larger than that in any house. The ceiling was the highest in town. If the mako could be persuaded to leap up into the air-filled room, fall on the floor, and be unable to get out again, it would die.

The hotel manager might not like the idea, but Roger wasn't going to ask the hotel manager.

How could he draw the shark inside? He himself must be the bait. He dropped through the great door into the water and swam out where the shark could see him. It immediately stopped trying to nose its way in through the window and swam under the hotel after the boy. Roger was only a few feet ahead of it when he clambered up into the lobby.

The shark soared up like a rocket and collapsed on the floor. Any guests left in the lobby lost no time in making themselves scarce. The big room was left to Roger and the shark.

Roger felt the flush of victory. This was the end of the killer of Undersea City. Now people could come and go in peace —or would be able to as soon as the beast died. That would not take long. Roger made himself comfortable in an easy chair and waited for it to happen.

It didn't happen. The shark began to squirm and twist, and its tail, still down in the water, thrashed about violently, drawing the body inch by inch back through the hole. As Roger watched helplessly, the mako dropped through into the sea and swam away.

The disappointed hunter went home.

"Did you get it?" said Hal.

"No luck," Roger said. "I'm going to try laser. Why didn't we think of that before?"

"Because it's not worth thinking about," Hal said. "Our laser is a small outfit. It will kill fish as big as marlin or grouper or sailfish, but it wouldn't have any effect on a twenty-five-foot shark. I think you've done about all you can in this little contest and you'll have to admit that the mako is the winner."

"And I suppose you'll say, 'I told you so,' " Roger said bitterly.

"I'll say no such thing. I think you've put up a good fight and you shouldn't be ashamed because a twenty-five-foot beast was too much for a five-foot boy."

But Roger was not ready to give up. He racked his brain. There must be a way to get the better of that rascal. Then a spark of fire came into his eyes.

"I'm going to try one more thing," he said, and dropped through the door.

He went again into Main Street and entered a shop advertising "Miner's Supplies." The walls were covered with the tools of mining—picks, pans, shovels, drills, instruments for measuring gravity and electrical discharges, magnetometers, gravimeters, and spectroscopes. But Roger didn't see what he wanted.

"Don't you have explosives?"

"Of course," said the clerk. "We keep them locked up. But we don't sell them to boys. What is it you want an explosive for?"

"To explode."

"To explode what? Copper ore, lead, tin—what?"

"A shark," Roger said.

The clerk stared. "A shark?"

"The one that is killing people in this town."

The clerk hesitated. "It all sounds very irregular," he said. "Have you any authority?"

"Call up Dr. Dick," Roger suggested.

The clerk went to the phone. He got Dr. Dick on the wire. "There's a boy here who wants explosives to blow up a shark."

"Who is it?" Dr. Dick asked.

The clerk turned to Roger. "What's your name?"

"Roger Hunt."

"His name is Roger Hunt," said the clerk over the phone.

"Let him have anything he wants," said Dr. Dick.

The clerk hung up and turned to Roger. "Why didn't you tell me your name was Hunt? Everybody here knows what you and your brother have been doing." He opened his safe. It was full of deadly-looking contraptions. He took out what appeared to be a steel ball with a clock in its side.

"I suppose your shark won't stay still and wait to be exploded. So you won't have a chance to plug in at any electrical outlet. You'll need something automatic—like this. Set the clock ahead and you'll have time to get out of the way before it goes off."

"Just the thing," Roger said. "What do I owe you?"

"Not a red cent. That shark killed two friends of mine. If we can help you get rid of it, we're only too glad to do so." He put the ball into a waterproof sack and handed it to his young customer.

Roger went next to a butcher shop. "I want a chunk of meat big enough so I can put this inside of it."

The butcher was bewildered. He had never had an order like this before. "Well, I don't know. Let me see. It would fall out of most anything you could put it into. Except—how about a suckling pig? You could jam that thing down its throat and it would stay in."

"Fine," Roger said.

The butcher brought out the carcass of a small pig from the freezer. Roger went out with the ball under one arm and the pig under the other.

The butcher looked after him and shook his head. "Crazy as a loon," he said.

Roger had to wait half an hour before he saw the shark slowly approaching down Main Street. He acted fast. He laid the pig in the middle of the street where the shark could not fail to notice it. He did not need to remove the watertight bag from the ball because it was transparent and he could see the control for setting the clock. He moved it to a five-minute delay. Then he jammed it, bag and all, down the small throat of the pig into the large stomach.

Other people had already scurried to safety and Roger now did the same. He watched from a shop window.

The man-eater lazied down the street looking for a victim. It saw the pig, swooped down, and swallowed it at one gulp.

Roger looked at the watertight watch on his wrist. Two minutes of the five had already gone by. He hoped the shark would wander on down the middle of the street where the explosion could not injure any person or damage a building.

But the big fish was not moving away. It nosed about, evidently hunting for another juicy bit like the one it had just enjoyed. Only three minutes were left before that thing would go off.

If the shark had stayed out in the open, Roger would not have been worried. He became nervous when he saw the beast edging over toward the buildings. Only two minutes now. The creature explored the ground under the butcher shop. Only one minute was left.

The shark moved next door under the shop where Roger and others had taken refuge. Roger was sorry he had ever started this thing. If people were killed, it would be his fault. He would never forgive himself, nor would anybody else forgive him. He could feel the cold sweat running down his back.

Only fifty seconds now, then forty, then thirty. How strong was that explosive? Would it blow up the building and kill all the occupants? Twenty seconds.

Failing to find any more pigs, the shark idly swam out again into the street. With a dull thud the charge went off. The effect was immediate. The man-eater of Undersea City turned upside down and slowly sank to the bottom. A hole as big as a barrel was torn in the white hide that had been too tough for knives, spears, or bullets.

Men began to grope through the hole for the valuable parts that may make a big shark worth seven thousand dollars.

Out came the great liver, eight feet long and weighing well up toward a hundred pounds. From it would come a valuable oil and vitamins A and D.

The hide would make excellent leather. The teeth would be used for razors, weapons, and surgical instruments. They would also be fashioned into costume jewelry. The fins could be sent to China to make the famous shark's-fin soup. The cartilage (the shark has no true bones) would become a high-protein food. The air bladders could be made into isinglass for gelatine or glue. The great jaws were taken by the proprietor of the Undersea City curio store. Indeed, as was once said of the hog, everything about the shark is usable but his breath.

The heart was pulled out, and it lay, still beating, in the hands of the man who had found it. That is one of the amazing things about this amazing animal—the heart keeps on going after the fish is dead. A. Hyatt Verrill, noted sailor and author, reported that the heart removed from a fifteen-foot tiger shark captured at Silver Shoals throbbed steadily as it was passed from man to man. Even after it was tossed on the deck, it continued to beat for more than an hour until the blazing sun dried and shriveled its surface.

It is really not so astonishing, after all, when we remember that a snake may wriggle long after it is dead, and the piranha of the Amazon after its head has been cut off will continue to snap its murderous jaws.

One thing about the shark remained really alive. This was a remora, or suckerfish, which is in the habit of clamping its vacuum mouth on the hide of a large fish and taking a free ride. But what made it more extraordinary in this case was that the remora was inside the shark's mouth, glued to the tongue. It was pulled away and given to a small boy who took it home to have it cooked for supper.

How about the eight people who had been killed by this villain? No trace of them was found. Even the bones were gone. The shark's powerful stomach acids can dissolve bones in a few hours.

However, there was plenty of proof of the monster's guilt. Among the shark's stomach contents were not only bottles, cans, chunks of wood and scrap iron, but bracelets, necklaces, long hair, a pair of eyeglasses, and many other articles that had been worn by the shark's victims.

A woman recognized a large hunting knife that had belonged to her husband. She seized it, then hastily dropped it, as if she had been burned. The hydrochloric acid in the shark's digestive juices is so powerful that it will promptly scorch human flesh that happens to touch it. The woman wrapped the knife in a piece of seaweed, then sadly took it home.

The flesh of the shark was cut into chunks which the mayor distributed to workmen from the South Sea Islands who did not share the Americans' distaste for shark meat.

One of the hotel's lady guests who had been watching all this bloody business seemed to be very weak in the knees. She turned to go back to the hotel. The mayor of Undersea City noticed that she alone was leaving with empty hands. He must give her something. He pressed into her hands the big heart, still palpitating.

The lady looked as if she were about to faint. She could not offend the mayor by refusing the gift. She gingerly carried it through the crowd, a painful smile on her face.

An island woman looked at the heart as if she would like

to have it. The nervous visitor was only too glad to get rid of it. She gave it to the woman who happily carried it home. It would probably beat until it was time to cook it for dinner. It was hard to get fresh meat in Undersea City, and what could be fresher than this?

Gold!

Hal sat alone in the glass jeep, superintending his "cowboys" —the dolphins who were guarding the lobster farm.

They circled the field, keeping off marauders, large fish that considered lobsters a very dainty meal. Even sharks feared the swift attacks and sharp teeth of the dolphins.

Hal saw a bumpfish at work. This was a rare specimen. He must get it. The bumpfish has a very hard head like the bumper of an automobile. The bumpfish dives swiftly at a coral block and hits it so powerfully that a piece of the coral is broken off. It then chews up the coral, not because it likes coral, but because the small living polyps in the coral are its favorite food.

This bumpfish was breaking off pieces of coral as big as a fist and chewing them up to get at the tiny animals inside.

Hal slipped out of the jeep, swam down very quietly so that the fish would not notice him, grabbed it and popped it into a plastic bag full of seawater. He returned to the jeep and settled down to examine his prize.

The fish swam about madly. It was so excited that it spilled the ground-up coral from its mouth. Hal was startled to see among the grains of coral other sparkling grains that looked very much like gold.

He looked again at the hump of coral on the sea floor where the fish had been feasting. Why had the little coral animals chosen this place to build their homes? It was mostly covered with sand. The fish must have pushed some of the sand aside to get at the coral. What had made this little hill? Was there a rock under the coral? Or just a heap of sand?

He turned on the laser and directed the beam at the curious hump. Immediately the dial on the machine showed that there was really something very hard down there.

With his laser beam he explored the edge of the hard thing for about a hundred feet. Then there was no more of it. He came back on the other side until he reached the other end.

The thing had the shape of a ship. It must be a ship. That was not strange. These were dangerous waters. Many ships had been lost in the Coral Sea off the Great Barrier Reef.

But why the gold?

Then he remembered Australia's great Gold Rush of a century ago. Ships had flocked to Australia from all over the world. In a single year nearly a hundred million dollars' worth of gold had been taken in ships bound for Europe or America. Some of the vessels never finished the trip. They sank in the storms of the Great Barrier Reef. They could not be salvaged. In those days divers could not descend to such depths.

Almost breathless with excitement, Hal went down with a hammer and knocked off pieces of coral. Every piece showed those golden glints. This was gold dust. The sacks in which it had been stored had long since rotted away, and the dust was scattered in the sand and became part of the growing coral.

He struck deeper and came upon a solid bar of gold about a foot long. Then he found another, and another. This was too much. He felt dizzy. He took an armful of bars and swam up to the jeep. At this depth the bars were no heavier than sticks of wood. But when he tried to lift them into the jeep, they showed their real weight.

He phoned Captain Ted in the *Flying Cloud* above.

"Let down the vac. I've found something pretty wonderful."

He impatiently waited until the big vacuum tube sank down.

"Turn on the power," he telephoned.

"What's coming up?" inquired Captain Ted.

"Sand."

"And you call that wonderful?"

"No. But we have to get rid of the sand before we can get at what's beneath."

"And what's beneath?"

"Gold."

"Thundering fishhooks," exclaimed the captain.

When the sand was cleared away, what was left of the wreck was plainly visible. During the century since it had gone to the bottom much of it had rotted and disappeared. The strongly built bulwarks and keel were still there. The sacks that had contained the gold dust had melted away during the century underwater and so had the chests or boxes in which the gold bars had been packed. But all that didn't matter. The important thing was that the bars were still there.

Hal wondered what he should do. Should he go at once and report to Dr. Dick? Why should he? He was not working for Dr. Dick now, he was on his own. The wreck did not lie within the limits of Undersea City. It was a good two miles out of town.

These were Australian waters. Any treasure found there belonged half to the man who discovered it and half to the Australian government.

Should he notify Australian officials and have them send an inspector to examine this fortune on the bottom of the sea and make arrangements to take away the share belonging to the government?

He knew that governments work slowly. It might be days or even weeks before an inspector would arrive, then more days or weeks before a vessel would be sent for the gold.

But during all that time the gold would be exposed to view and thieves might steal it. He was still pondering this problem when he saw one of Undersea City's small subs approaching. He recognized it as the runabout used by the Reverend Merlin Kaggs. It passed close. Kaggs waved to him, then went on.

Hal breathed more easily. Kaggs hadn't noticed what lay on the sea floor, Hal thought. But he was mistaken.

Kaggs had seen just enough to make him curious. The little sub returned. It went down and circled around the wreck. Then it rose and passed out of sight.

Hal knew what he must do. Since he didn't trust Kaggs, he must put his gold where it would not be a temptation to Kaggs or anyone else. He must load it on the *Flying Cloud.* There Captain Ted and his crew would guard it until the arrival of a government inspector.

How would he get the bars up to the ship? A dolphin could tow them, but only a few at a time. It was really a job for Big Boy, the killer whale. The whale was usually to be found near the house.

Hal drove back to the house and told Roger what he had seen. The boy's eyes popped.

"Gee—I want to see it. I'm going back with you."

"Fine," Hal said. "You can help me."

"Have you told Dr. Dick about it?"

"I don't need to," Hal said. "But I think I will anyhow."

He got Dr. Dick on the phone and described the wreck and its cargo.

"Where is it?" Dick asked.

"About two miles out."

"Well—thank you for telling me about it. But it's really none of my business. That's outside of our territory. And remember, you're working for yourself now, not for us. Good luck," and he rang off.

Hal said. "That man is as honest as the day is long."

Hal and Roger returned to the wreck, followed by the whale.

As they neared the wreck they saw that somebody else was there. A one-man sub hovered over the place and Kaggs himself stood on a bulwark of the old ship looking at the gold. A few sharks held off from the lobster farm by the dolphins passed over his head. He was so occupied in gloating over the treasure that he did not notice them.

Suddenly one of the sharks, perhaps bad-tempered because it could not get at the lobsters, dropped and closed its jaws on his shoulder.

"Come on!" said Hal. He and Roger dropped out of the jeep and swam to the rescue of the unfortunate missionary. Blood from his shoulder was turning the water pink. His mouthpiece had dropped from his mouth, and if the shark did not kill him, he would die by drowning.

Roger had already learned that he had little chance of puncturing a shark with a knife or spear or even a bullet. But he knew that the most tender spot on a shark is the end of the nose. The beast couldn't be killed by poking its nose, but many a diver had driven off a shark by swatting it with a club on the end of the snout.

Roger had no club. He picked up a gold bar and with all his strength hit the creature on its most tender spot.

The shark dropped Kaggs and swam away. The missionary sagged to the ground, unconscious. A few moments more without air and he would drown. Hal took him by the head, Roger took him by the feet, and between them they got him up to the jeep and inside. Hal pumped the water out of him and gave him first aid. He began to breathe. Slowly he came alive. He opened his eyes. He looked dully at Hal and Roger. He still did not realize what had happened.

Then he noticed his own bloody shoulder, and remembered.

"That beast almost did for me. Guess I owe my life to you."

He closed his eyes for a time, then opened them and said, "Why did you do it? After what I did to you on the desert island, why did you stop that shark from making a meal on me?"

Hal was dressing the injured shoulder with antiseptic and salve.

"I don't know," he said. "We must have thought you were worth saving."

"That was generous of you," said Kaggs. He took Hal's hand in one of his and Roger's in the other. "Now we are friends, yes? All the past is forgotten, yes?"

"Yes," Hal said.

Roger did not say either yes or no.

"I see you found some treasure," Kaggs said. "What are you going to do with it?"

"Take it upstairs," said Hal.

"To your ship?"

"That's right."

"I'll help you," Kaggs said. "That's the best way I know to show you how I feel about you."

"You'd better rest a while longer."

"No, no. I'm all right now. Let's get going."

The boys would have been just as glad not to have Kaggs's

help. But the fellow seemed so anxious to prove that he was their friend, they could not refuse him.

Hal phoned Captain Ted. "Keep an eye out for the whale. He'll be bringing up the bars. Hoist them aboard and stow them in the hold."

Then Hal, Roger, and Kaggs descended to the wreck. Hal carried a stout rope. Big Boy, seeing the rope, guessed that this was going to be a job for him and came close.

One end of the rope was looped around his neck and the other end was tied around a half ton of bars. The load was easily pulled to the surface by the powerful whale, and the crane of the *Flying Cloud* lifted it aboard.

The job was repeated time and time again until every bar that could be found had been transferred to the ship.

Kaggs returned to his sub and with a final friendly wave to the boys, sped away.

Hal and Roger returned to the glass jeep. Hal phoned the captain. "That's all of it, Ted. Next thing is to get an inspector. This phone won't reach Cairns but yours will. Phone the chief of police in Cairns and ask him to telephone Brisbane for an inspector."

"And I hope he comes soon," the captain complained. "Do you realize this ship is almost awash, that stuff is so heavy. If we had a spell of bad weather right now, we might go to the bottom."

Murder Will Out

The next morning Dr. Dick had a caller. He was a young man, brown-skinned, evidently a Polynesian.

"Sit down," said Dr. Dick cordially. "What can I do for you?"

"My name is Taro," said the young stranger. "I'm from an island up north. It's called Ponape."

"I know the island," said Dr. Dick. "What brings you here?"

"Looking for a job. I came about a week ago. I was hired by the mining engineer. Yesterday I went to church. I recognized the preacher."

"Ah, the Reverend Mr. Kaggs. You had seen him before?"

"Yes, on Ponape. I was wondering if you knew about him."

"What is there to know?"

"What sort of man he really is."

"Well, I know only what he told me. He's been a missionary in the South Sea Islands for years."

"He's no missionary," Taro said. "He's a murderer and a pearl thief. He was in prison for a long spell after he committed two murders. Then he pretended that he had reformed. He changed his name and called himself the Reverend Archibald Jones. He went about quoting passages from the Bible and stealing everything he could lay his hands on. He shot a friend of mine. He went with two boys to a desert island, then sailed away and left them there to die. They barely escaped with their lives. I thought you ought to know about these things. I didn't believe you would have hired him if you had known."

Dr. Dick studied Taro's face. He looked honest, but how could you tell? The Polynesians were very imaginative people. Perhaps none of this had really happened. Taro might be making up the whole story.

He said to Taro, "I hope you are aware that you have been making some very serious charges. I will investigate your story. If it is true, you are to be thanked for telling me. If it is not true, you will be discharged."

"Fair enough," Taro said.

After he had gone Dr. Dick phoned Kaggs. "If you aren't busy, could you drop over to see me for a few moments?"

"Certainly," said Kaggs. "It happens to be my hour for prayer and meditation and I have a sermon to prepare for next Sunday. But I shall be able to give you a few minutes."

When he came, Dr. Dick said, "Sorry to interrupt your spiritual duties. When you came to us, did you tell us all about yourself?"

Kaggs was startled. "I don't know what you mean. Of course I told you everything that I thought would interest you."

"You told me about your long missionary service in the islands. You told me how you had brought the Gospel to the ignorant heathen of the South Seas. By the way, did you ever meet the Reverend Archibald Jones?"

Kaggs stared. "Wh-wh-why," he stuttered, "the name is

not familiar. I don't think I've ever had the pleasure of meeting the gentleman."

"Well, you may have the pleasure now. I will tell you about him. He looks very much like you. But he had an unfortunate past. He committed two murders, and spent many years in prison. When he was released he changed his name, came to the islands, and went about like a missionary preaching to the people. Since you were also a missionary in the islands, I should think you would have met him—especially when you looked in the mirror."

An angry flush spread over Kaggs's face. "Who told you this?" he demanded.

"That's not important. The important question is just this: Is it true?"

Kaggs saw that it was hopeless to deny it. Dr. Dick had the facts.

"It's true," Kaggs admitted. "And what of it? It's not the first time that a man has made mistakes and gone to prison. It's not the first time that a man has come out of prison determined to make a better life. Such a man should be given a chance. He has paid for the wrongs he has done. Prison has given him time to think. It has given him time to read his Bible and resolve to pattern his life according to the teachings in that book. I came out of prison a changed man. I wanted only to do good. My only desire was to be a blessing to the poor and needy natives of the South Seas. I became a missionary and have been doing good ever since."

Dr. Dick smiled. "That all sounds very fine. Certainly a man who has paid for his wrongdoing deserves another chance. But if you had become such a holy man, how did it happen that you went about stealing from the very natives you preached to? Had you really changed? How about the new crimes you committed?"

"What crimes?"

"You planned the murder of two young men. You left them on an uninhabited island where you thought they would die of hunger and thirst. You shot a Ponapean. I have no doubt it was you who made the landslide down the face of the Great Barrier Reef that almost killed our two naturalists. Are all these acts the acts of a man who has changed?"

Kaggs rose from his chair, shaking his fist. "You tell me who put you wise to all this or I'll push your face in."

"Try it," said Dr. Dick. "You will leave this house quietly. Your services as the pastor of the church of Undersea City are no longer required. You will get out of town and never come back."

"Who told you?" shouted Kaggs.

"That's none of your business."

"It is my business. Never mind—I know who it was. And he'll pay for it." He stormed out.

He started toward the house he shared with Hal and Roger. Hal must be the one who had blabbed to Dr. Dick. Probably his brother was in it, too. Kaggs would kill both of them.

But before he got around the corner into Barracuda Street he had cooled down a bit. He had seen the strength and courage of both of these young men. He was no match for the two of them. Even if Hal was there alone, he dared not fight him. He would have to think of another way to get back at these two tattletales.

Then he thought of the *Flying Cloud*, loaded to the gunwales with rare fish worth a hundred thousand dollars, and gold bars of untold value, perhaps millions.

So when he entered the house, he was all sweetness and light. He cheerily greeted the boys.

"What did Dr. Dick want?" Hal asked.

"He just wanted to thank me for yesterday's sermon. He

said it gave him great spiritual comfort. He wanted to increase my salary. I declined to accept more. I am here not for money, but for the good I can do."

He went into his room. He came out in a few minutes carrying a bag.

"You look as if you are about to travel," Hal said.

"No, no. Just going to the church."

"Why the bag?" Roger asked.

"Bibles," responded Kaggs. "Bibles for my people. Would you believe it—many of my parishioners have no Bible."

He smiled his way out.

"Not such a bad guy after all," Hal said.

Roger shook his head. "I think he has something up his sleeve."

Kaggs with his bag of personal belongings—and no Bibles —boarded his little sub. He knew that going up would be slow. Any sudden climb would bring on the bends.

He went up fifty feet and stopped. The open hatch allowed some of the helium air to escape and his body slowly adapted itself to less pressure. For a long time he waited, impatient to get on before his trick was discovered.

At last he climbed another fifty feet and stopped again.

The third time he was only fifty feet from the surface. When he had finally fretted through another long delay, he rose to the surface, sighted the *Flying Cloud*, and steered for the rope ladder that hung from its rail. He came out of the sub, abandoning it to float wherever it chose, and climbed to the deck.

There was no one to be seen.

He went down the companionway to the captain's cabin and knocked on the door. He heard a gruff "Come in." He took a revolver from his bag, opened the door, and went in.

The captain, seeing the gun, reached for his own. A blast of Kaggs's gun stopped him. Kaggs had taken care to miss. He would need the captain to navigate the ship.

Captain Ted recognized the fellow. Hal had described him. "You're Merlin Kaggs. What do you want?"

"Just behave," said Kaggs, "unless you think you'd look good without a head. Up on deck with you and get under way."

"Can't do that," said Captain Ted. "My men aren't here."

"Where are they?"

"Went fishing up the reef."

"All the better," said Kaggs. "That makes two less that I'll have to shoot."

"You think I can run this ship all by myself?"

"Don't worry, I'll help you. I was mate once on a tub like this. Move."

The captain climbed to the deck, Kaggs close behind.

"Where to?" said Captain Ted.

"Some quiet cove north of Cairns. Where I can get this stuff ashore without disturbing the police. But near the railroad."

The captain looked up at the idly flapping sails. "No use," he said. "The wind is wrong."

"Don't give me that," growled Kaggs. "The wind's okay. Besides, you have an auxiliary engine."

The captain looked Kaggs up and down. "You really expect to get away with this? You evidently know what we have aboard. Don't you realize that half of it belongs to the Australian government? You could be slapped in jail for the rest of your life for making off with government property. Unless you are killed first by the Hunts."

Kaggs laughed. "I'm not afraid of either the government or the Hunts. How can two boys stop me? I've killed before, I can kill again. But I won't need to. They'll know nothing about this until it's too late. We've gabbled too long—now get busy."

"First," said Captain Ted, "you'll have to go forward and get up the anchor."

Kaggs went forward. The captain sidled toward the phone on the bulkhead. The Hunts were going to know right now what had happened. Before he could reach the instrument Kaggs wheeled about and fired. The phone lay in fragments on the deck.

"I hope you understand now that I know how to handle this," said Kaggs, tapping his gun. "Last time I shot at you I missed—on purpose. Next time I may not miss. I can run this scow alone if I have to. Any more monkey business, and I'll do just that. Remember, I'm the boss—you're only the captain."

With the anchor up and the sails set, the little ship began to move.

"Not fast enough," Kaggs said. "Turn on the engine."

"It's not safe to go too fast," the captain warned. "There are a lot of reefs ahead."

"I'm giving the orders," roared Kaggs. "Get going."

Ted dropped down into the engine room and did as he was told. There was a passage leading from the engine room to his cabin. He went to the cabin and sat down before the logbook. He would put a report of this affair into the log so that if anything happened to him there would be written evidence to show who had stolen the ship and murdered him.

The door opened and Kaggs came in.

"What are you up to?" he demanded. He looked over the captain's shoulder and saw his own name. "Still playing tricks," he said. "Get up on deck—quick."

Kaggs grabbed the log and followed the captain to the deck. He went to the rail, opened the book, tore the first sheet into two parts and threw them into the sea. He went on, tearing up and tossing away every leaf. The captain suffered in silence. Nothing is so sacred to the master of a vessel as his log.

When the two missing men returned from their fishing trip, their ship was not where it had been moored. Had it sunk because of the great weight of its cargo? They saw the scraps of paper on the sea. They picked up one of them and examined it. It was a piece of the ship's log. The row of scraps led northeast. It was plain that the ship had sailed away in that direction.

"Tom, whatever do you think could have happened?"

"It's clear enough," said Tom. "All that treasure aboard was too much of a temptation for him. He's made off with the ship."

"Who? You don't mean the captain."

"Who else?" said Tom. "He was the only one aboard."

"I never would have believed he'd do a thing like that."

"I know. But what else can you believe?"

"Well, I believe we've got to get word to Hal Hunt right away."

"How can we do that? Do you think we have a phone in this dinghy? Hunt is two hundred feet down. We have no aqualungs. I can't swim that deep without a tank and neither can you."

The other scanned the horizon. "There she is." About three miles off lay the ship of the Undersea Science Foundation, the *Discovery*. "They have a phone. We're lucky that the ship is downwind."

He jibbed the sail and let out the sheet to get the full benefit of the breeze. The little boat sped toward the *Discovery*. On board, they found the captain.

"We're from the *Flying Cloud*," Tom said.

"Nice to have you, boys. Make yourselves at home."

"No, this is not a social call. Our ship is gone. Did you see it leave?"

"No. We were busy below decks." He raised his binoculars and searched the sea where the ship had been.

"We want to phone Hal Hunt," Tom said.

"Yes, you'd better do that. Phone's right over there."

Hal was stunned by the news. "Can't understand it," he said. "Why did the captain sail off without telling me?"

"Perhaps something happened to the phone," suggested Roger, never dreaming how close he was to the truth. "All that gold and stuff. You don't suppose Captain Ted . . ."

"Don't be ridiculous. I'd stake my life on that man."

"Where's Kaggs?" said Roger. "He was just going to the church. He should have been back long ago."

Hal thought of the bag that was supposed to be full of Bibles. And he thought of the *Flying Cloud*'s hull, full of gold. It didn't take any great feat of arithmetic to put the two together. "Kaggs! That rascal!"

He phoned Dr. Dick. "Our ship is gone. We think it must have been stolen."

"Stolen! Who could have . . ." Then he thought of the murderer and thief he had fired that morning. "I can guess," he said. "What can I do for you?"

"We want to go after it. May we borrow the hoversub?"

"Right away. It will be in front of your house in five minutes."

The Chase

It was there in less than five. The same pilot who had taken them to the Mariana Trench was at the controls.

It was not necessary to stop on the way up for decompression, since the sub was charged with the same helium they had been breathing below, and at the same pressure. The hatch was closed and they shot upward.

Reaching the surface, the hoversub leaped into the air like an acrobatic whale and skimmed along twelve feet above the sea supported by its column of down-rushing air.

"It was just about here that she lay," Hal said. "I wonder if we can get any idea what direction she took."

He looked for bubbles left by the wake of the ship. But they had long since disappeared. Then he noticed the scraps of paper.

"Look," he said to the pilot. "Follow those. He wasn't heading for Brisbane or Sydney. This line would take him to one of the deserted bays north of Cairns. Smugglers use them to get their stolen goods ashore. If we find the ship, we'll be landing on the surface. Ease the pressure out of this thing very slowly so that by the time we get there it will be the same as the air pressure."

When there was no more paper to be seen, the pilot looked at his compass and held the hoversub to exactly the same direction. The *Magic Carpet* sped over water, reefs, sand spits, and coral islands with equal ease. The ship, of course, had been compelled to go around these bits of land, so by now it might be a little to one side or the other of the compass course. The pilot kept watch ahead, Hal out the right window, and Roger out the left.

Things were not going too well on board the *Flying Cloud*. Captain Ted made another brave effort to take back his ship from the pirate Kaggs.

When Kaggs was not looking, the captain picked up a belaying pin. This was like the heavy club used by the police. He stepped up quietly behind Kaggs and brought the weapon down with terrific force.

Kaggs moved his head just in time, and the belaying pin did nothing but graze his right temple and cheek, bringing the blood.

He wheeled about and struck out with both fists, one landing under Ted's jaw and the other in his solar plexus. The stunned captain fell to the deck, unconscious. Before he could come to, Kaggs seized a coil of rope and tied him up, hand and foot. "There," he said triumphantly, "now he'll give me no more trouble."

He had no sooner spoken the words than there was a grinding sound beneath his feet and the vessel shuddered to a stop. It had run up onto a reef.

He had thought that he knew how to handle a ship. But he had never had this experience before. How do you get a ship off a reef?

He shook the captain. "Wake up, you son of a gun. Wake up and do something."

It was no use. He must do something himself. The wind pressing on the sails was pushing the ship inch by inch farther up on the jagged coral. The razor-sharp edges of coral were sawing into the hull. A bubbling sound beneath told him that one of the strakes had been broken and seawater was coming in.

He kicked the unconscious captain. He wished he had not punched him quite so hard. Well, the first thing to do was to get down the sails. He did this, then went down and turned off the engine. Now he hoped the ship would slide back into deep water. It did not. He turned on the engine, and put it in reverse. That should pull her off. But she did not move. The water was sloshing around Kaggs's feet.

The water ought to be pumped out. Did the ship have a pump, and if so where was it?

He went up and gave the captain a rousing kick. Ted opened his eyes.

"Get up, you lazy beggar. We're stuck on a reef."

A faint smile came over the captain's face.

"Don't forget," he said. "You're the boss. Get it off." He closed his eyes and seemed to go to sleep.

Kaggs realized that the captain could not help him so long as his hands and feet were bound. He got down and began to untie the knots. Then he tied them tighter than before. So long as this fellow was tied up he couldn't get into mischief.

Kaggs had another idea. The gold. The hull was full of it. It was very heavy. If it were thrown overboard . . .

The idea made him sick. Had he gone through all this just to lose the treasure after all? But he could think of nothing else to do.

He was so occupied that he hardly noticed something leap

out of the sea, perhaps a whale or a marlin. He went down into the hold. He looked sadly at the tremendous store of gold bars. He could live beautifully the rest of his life on this fortune. It would all have been his if he hadn't been so careless as to let the ship run aground.

Oh, well, there was nothing to do but get rid of it. He gathered as many as he could carry and staggered up the companionway. There seemed to be a shadow above him. He looked up and saw Hal and Roger waiting for him.

So that thing leaping out of the sea—it had not been a whale or a fish. Kaggs dropped the gold bars and they clattered down the steps. He began to reach for his gun. He was stopped by a sharp command, "Hold it!" It came from the captain, freed by the boys, and now standing with a ready gun in his hands.

Kaggs knew when to be tough and when to be sweet. He smiled pleasantly. "I was just trying to save your ship," he said. He came up on deck.

"So that's your idea of how to save it," Hal said. "Steal it and then run it on a reef. What will we do with him, Captain?"

"Put him in the brig. It's in the fo'c'sle."

The brig was an iron cage in which trouble-making sailors could be locked up. Kaggs was introduced to his new quarters and the key turned in the lock.

"That will take care of him," Hal said, "until we get the police. Where's the phone?"

"There it is," said Captain Ted, pointing to the broken pieces on the deck. "I'm afraid we'll have to forget the police for a while. The first thing to do is to get the ship off. The tide is rising. As soon as it's high, perhaps she'll float. In the meantime I'll turn on the pump and get rid of some of this water."

But at high tide the schooner was still fast on the coral.

"We need an anchor astern," the captain said, "but we have no dinghy to carry it out."

"*Magic Carpet* can do that," Hal suggested. He looked for the hoversub. It was gone. The pilot was already speeding it back to Undersea City.

"Roger and I will take it out," Hal suggested. They stripped and swam aft about a hundred feet with the anchor. There they dropped it and swam back to the ship.

Ted already had the electric capstan turning, tightening the line on the anchor. That should gradually drag the ship back off the reef.

The line to the anchor tightened more and more until it was as taut as a bowstring. The ship gritted its teeth on the coral which cut a larger hole in the bottom. Suddenly the line to the anchor snapped in two.

All they had done was to lose an anchor.

The ship had been dragged back just far enough to make the situation worse. Now the hole was not half choked by the reef, but in deeper water so that the hold was filling faster than ever. More water came in than the pump could take out. If this went on, the ship would slide off the reef, only to sink stern first.

Roger's thoughts were far away. He was thinking about Captain Cook. Captain Cook, the great navigator who had discovered Australia, had his ship run aground in exactly the same way close to this very same place. He had saved his ship. Roger remembered how he had done it.

"Let's fother it," he said suddenly.

Captain Ted had not read much history. He smiled indulgently. What was this nonsense?

"What do you mean—fother?"

"Captain Cook did it. Why can't we? Have you got an old sail around the place?"

"Over there—in the locker."

Roger got it and spread it out on the deck.

"How about some tar?" Roger asked.

Captain Ted was getting annoyed. "What is all this nonsense?"

But Hal now remembered what Captain Cook had done. "The kid's on the right track. Let him have the tar."

He helped Roger smear the tar thickly over the canvas.

Then they carried it aft and let it down over the stern. They drew it up under the hull so that it covered the hole.

The pressure of the sea pushed the tarred sail up against the hole so firmly that the inflow of water was shut off.

"Well I'll be hornswoggled," said Captain Ted. "I've sailed these seas for fifty years, but I'm learning something new every day."

Safe Harbor

Now the pump could really do its work. Within an hour it had sucked up all the water in the hull and poured it overboard. With this load removed, the ship was several tons lighter than before.

The line from the capstan back to the anchor was repaired. At the next high tide the power was turned on in the electric capstan, the line tightened, the ship groaned and creaked over the coral and was drawn back over the reef into deep water.

Captain Ted went down into the hold. He came back, beaming.

"It works. Not a drop of water coming in. That Cook fellow was pretty smart. Now, where do you want to go? On to Smuggler's Bay?"

"No," Hal said. "What's the nearest port with inspectors, a good bank, and a dry dock where we can get the hull repaired?"

"That would be Brisbane," said Captain Ted. "Perhaps you can help me get these sails up."

The breeze was good and the ship sped away on its new course. Roger clambered up the ratlines to the crow's nest. His keen eyes searched the sea for reefs. The ones above the surface were easy to see. But there were many others underwater. They might be far enough down so that the ship could pass over them, or they might be only two or three feet below the surface. These he could not see, but he could spot them by the color of the water. Deep water was a deep blue, shallow water was a light blue or tan or coral-pink. When he saw one of these danger tints ahead, he would shout down to Captain Ted at the wheel and the course would be altered to go around the reef.

These waters were much too perilous to be crossed at night. So when darkness came on, the ship was moored in the lee of a small island and the sails furled.

In the morning the first light found the *Flying Cloud* on its way again to Brisbane. The ship finally circled the last island and entered Moreton Bay.

"Here we are," Captain Ted announced.

Roger scanned the shore. He had expected to see a large city. He saw nothing but subtropical jungle—palms, flame trees, papaya, frangipani, orchid trees, and monster trees two hundred feet high that the captain called bunya bunyas.

"But where is Brisbane?" Roger wanted to know.

"Oh, we're not quite there yet. It's twenty-five miles up the Brisbane River. It's a twisty river, and dangerous. We'd better get down the sails and crawl up to town by engine."

The city, when they got to it, seemed very fine indeed.

"You'd never think it was founded by murderers and thieves," said Captain Ted. "That was more than a century ago. Britain had so many criminals she didn't have prisons big enough to take them all. So she shipped thousands of them out here. This was a very tough town in the beginning. But the sons and grandsons of the criminals grew up to be fine citizens and now this is one of the best cities in Australia. That's Kangaroo Point ahead. We can dock on the other side of it."

They had no sooner docked than Australian customs officials came aboard. They saw the tanks of fish. "What is this, a floating aquarium?"

"Some specimens we took off the Great Barrier Reef," Hal said.

"Do you expect to sell them here?"

"No. They will be transshipped to the United States. Will there be any duty on them?"

"No. We're not interested in fish. Do you have any other cargo?"

"Well," Hal said, "there are a few little items down below."

The men went below. They came back with their eyes fairly popping out of their heads.

"Do you realize you have a fortune down there?"

"Yes, we realize it," said Hal.

"What do you propose to do with it?"

"Give half of it to you—I mean to the Australian government. It's from a wreck. The wreck was in Australian waters, so Australia gets half of the gold. Can you appraise it?"

"No. That's taken care of by another department. We'll phone Government House for an inspector."

Hal was worried. He knew how slowly some governments act. "I hope it won't take too long," he said. "We don't want to stay here for more than a week or two."

Hal did not have to wait a week or two. The inspector arrived in fifteen minutes. Australia was not so slow after all. With the inspector were three police officers.

The inspector and police went below and saw the stacks upon stacks of gold bars.

The police noticed the man in the brig. One of the officers asked, "Who are you?"

"Just an unfortunate seaman."

"Why are you in here?"

"The captain put me here. He's a brute. You really ought to arrest him."

"What's your name?"

"John Smith."

The officers came up and one of them said, "Who's the captain of this ship?"

"I am," said Captain Ted.

"What has this John Smith done?"

"John Smith? Who's that?"

"The man in the brig. He says his name is John Smith."

Captain Ted laughed. "John Smith, says he? His name is Merlin Kaggs."

"Kaggs? Did you say Merlin Kaggs?"

"That's correct."

"We've been looking for a man by that name for the last eighteen months. He killed a pearl diver on Thursday Island. Then he disappeared. Where has he been all this time?"

"Meet Hal Hunt," said Captain Ted. "He can tell you all about him."

"He's been underwater," Hal said.

"What do you mean? What's he been doing?"

"He's been pastor of a church at the bottom of the sea."

"Look here," said one of the officers sternly. "This is serious business. Don't try to be funny."

"I'm not," said Hal. "Have you heard of Undersea City?"

"Seems to me I've read something about it. Is that where he's been hiding?"

"You've got it," Hal said.

"Did you know him well?"

"We lived in the same house with him."

"It's lucky he didn't try to kill you."

Hal smiled but said nothing.

"He *did* try to kill Hunt and his brother," said the captain, "by dumping a landslide on them from the Great Barrier Reef."

"Forget it," Hal said. "He's a little unbalanced up here." He tapped his head.

"All the more reason why he should be put away," said the officer. "But there's another thing and I'm afraid it involves you, Captain. We may have to book you on suspicion of having attempted grand theft."

Captain Ted's jaw dropped. "What have you got against me?"

"We have a plane that watches for any ships headed for Smuggler's Bay. Now that we see what cargo you were carrying, we have good reason to suppose that you were planning to land it there."

Hal spoke up. "You have it all wrong, officer. Kaggs stole the ship and tied up the captain. Kaggs hoped to unload the gold at Smuggler's Bay. But he wasn't too good a sailor. He ran the ship on a reef and punched a hole in the bottom. We caught up with him, untied the captain, and Kaggs was clapped into the brig. If your plane came around again, the pilot must have noticed that after we got under way we no longer headed for Smuggler's Bay but straight for Brisbane. And here we are—prepared to hand over half of the treasure to the Australian government. Doesn't that prove we weren't interested in any smuggling?"

The officer smiled. "You talk sense, young man." He shook hands with Hal, Roger, and the captain.

In the meantime the inspector had been making a careful examination of the treasure. He came up to say, "I can't make any estimate down there. You'll have to get these bars up and spread them out on the dock so I can make a count."

One of the police said, "I don't see why your friend Kaggs can't help you. Do you have the key to the brig?"

Captain Ted gave it to him. The three came up in a moment with the wriggling, ranting Kaggs, loudly protesting his innocence. He was told that he had to knuckle down and help bring up the bars.

"You don't know what you're asking," he said. "I'm no laborer. I'm a minister of the Gospel. I don't work with my hands."

"You don't work with your head either," said one of the officers, "or you wouldn't be in this mess. You're going to do hard labor in prison the rest of your life so you may as well get in a little practice now."

The two boys and the captain went to work bringing up bars. The inspector and police officers helped. Only Kaggs was sulky and unwilling. He refused to take part. An officer gave him a prod with his gun, and Kaggs changed his mind. As he went up and down an officer kept close to him, ready to use his gun if the criminal tried to escape.

When all the bars lay on the dock like a pavement of gold, the inspector made his count. Then he spoke to Hal.

"Forty-four hundred bars. That's twenty-two hundred for the government and the rest for you. This will have to be handled through a bank. What bank do you prefer?"

Hal said, "You know the Brisbane banks, I don't."

"I suggest the Queensland National," said the inspector. "It's the biggest, and it's close by. I'll telephone and see if they can send over a man."

What he said over the telephone must have been impressive, for the person who came was none other than the manager himself. He gasped when he saw the golden pavement.

"Verify my count," the inspector said. "Then cart this stuff away, have it appraised, divide the value in half, and give us two checks—one for the government and one made out to Hal Hunt."

"Not exactly," Hal said. "Don't make out a check to me. Kindly divide our half in two and write one check to the Undersea Science Foundation and the other to John Hunt and Sons."

"What's the big idea?" objected Captain Ted. "You found the treasure. Undersea City has no claim to any of it."

"That's the way I want it," Hal said. "I know my father would want it that way, too. They are doing a great work down there. They could do a lot more if they had more funds. My father is doing a wonderful job, too, protecting wild animals that might otherwise become as extinct as the dinosaur and the dodo. He can do even better with this help."

"Have it your own way," the banker said. "The bank's armored car will be here in a few minutes to pick this up."

One of the officers telephoned police headquarters for a patrol wagon. When it arrived, Kaggs was bundled into it and had a free ride to the jail. His last words to Hal were "When I get out, I'll have a score to settle with you."

There remained the job of transferring all the tanks of fishy treasures to a cargo vessel that would take them to the Hunt Animal Farm on Long Island. Then the *Flying Cloud* went into dry dock to get the hole in its hull patched up.

Hal cabled his father:

SPECIMENS COMING TO YOU BY MOTOR SHIP KANGAROO. LOOK ALSO FOR SLIP OF PAPER FROM QUEENSLAND NATIONAL BANK. WHAT DO YOU WANT US TO DO NOW? CABLE LENNON'S HOTEL BRISBANE.

It would take two or three days to get an answer, and about that long for repairs on the *Flying Cloud.*

The hotel seemed pretty luxurious after the simple quarters they had occupied at the bottom of the sea.

"And the food is better, too," Roger said, as they sat at a

table in the Rainbow Room listening to the orchestra and
absorbing kangaroo-tail soup, rock oysters on the half shell,
and baked Alaska.

Three days later they received John Hunt's answer:

DON'T KNOW EXACTLY WHAT YOU'VE BEEN UP TO BUT
AM PROUD OF YOU ANYHOW. WHAT DO YOU MEAN, SLIP
OF PAPER? I SUGGEST YOU EXPLORE WORLD'S WILDEST
ISLAND, NEW GUINEA. BUT LOOK OUT FOR CANNIBALS.
KEEP YOUR SHIP. WE NEED CROCODILES, SEA COWS, TI-
GER SHARKS, KOMODO DRAGONS, BIRDS OF PARADISE,
CASSOWARIES, KANGAROOS, BANDICOOTS, CUSCUS, FLY-
ING FOXES, PHALANGERS, GIANT SCORPIONS, DIONSAUR
LIZARDS, DEATH ADDERS, TAIPANS, KOALA BEARS,
CANNIBAL SKULLS FOR MUSEUMS.

Crocodile Adventure

Hal stared at his brother.

"That's the biggest job we've had yet," he said. "Wonder why he chose New Guinea."

"Because it's close by," Roger guessed. "Isn't it up at the end of the Great Barrier Reef?"

"Yes. Just off the north tip of Australia. But as different from Australia as a tiger is different from a lamb. I suppose it's the most dangerous place on earth for a kid like you to go roaming about. He expects me to take care of you. What does he think I am, a baby-sitter?"

Roger flushed. "I could poke you in the nose for that. What makes you think I can't take care of myself?"

Hal said, "You have a talent for getting into mischief."

"Well, don't I get myself out again?"

Hal thought about this. "Yes, I guess you do. But you've never had to face a pack of cannibals."

"Cannibals, my eye! Dad was just kidding about that. There aren't any cannibals anymore—anywhere. Don't Australians run New Guinea? They wouldn't allow headhunting there."

"They wouldn't if they could stop it," Hal agreed. "But it's not easy. Think what they're up against. New Guinea is the largest island on earth, except Greenland. And New Guinea is practically all mountains. High mountains, up to sixteen thousand feet. In most of the country there are no roads. Wild tribes are shut away in the mountain valleys. Many of these people have never seen a white man. How do you expect Australian patrols to police tribes they can't even reach?"

Roger objected. "But Dad wouldn't be sending us there if it weren't safe."

"He told us it wasn't safe," Hal retorted. "He said look out for cannibals. Well, I can't look out for cannibals and look out for you too. You can take a plane home and I'll go alone."

Roger was in a towering rage. "You send me home? Just try it. Don't forget—the name of our outfit is John Hunt and Sons. Sons, mind you, not Son. I'm part of the firm. I have the same rights as you. Besides you may need me to help you. Perhaps it'll be you, not me, who'll get into trouble."

Hal smiled. He realized that there was a man in this boy. "All right, I surrender," he said. "We'll stick together." He cabled his father:

ON OUR WAY TO NEW GUINEA

And what happened to them in the world's wildest island is told in *Crocodile Adventure.*

The reader is also invited to read *Amazon Adventure*, an account of the experiences of Hal and Roger on an expedition to collect wild animals in the Amazon jungle; *South Sea Adventure*, a story of pearls, a desert island, and a raft; *Underwater Adventure*, on the thrills of skin diving in tropic seas; *Volcano Adventure*, a story of a descent into the mountains of fire; *Whale Adventure*, about the monster that sank a ship; *African Adventure*, an exciting tale of the land of big game; *Elephant Adventure*, on a hazardous hunt in the Mountains of the Moon; *Safari Adventure*, on the war against poachers; *Lion Adventure*, on the capture of a man-eater; and *Gorilla Adventure*, on the life of a great ape.